THE PRIESTS OF PSI

and other stories

By the same author

THE PRIESTS OF PSI

and other stories

by

FRANK HERBERT

LONDON
VICTOR GOLLANCZ LTD
1980

ISBN 0 575 02778 9

ACKNOWLEDGMENTS

'Try to Remember' copyright © 1959 by *Renown* Publishing Corporation
'Old Rambling House' copyright © 1958 by The *Galaxy* Publishing Corporation
'Murder Will In' copyright © 1970 by Mercury Press, Inc.
'Mindfield' copyright © 1962 by The Ultimate Publishing Company
'The Priests of Psi' copyright © 1959 by The Ultimate Publishing Company

MADE AND PRINTED IN GREAT BRITAIN BY
THE GARDEN CITY PRESS LIMITED
LETCHWORTH, HERTFORDSHIRE
SG6 1JS

CONTENTS

TRY TO REMEMBER

Every mind on earth capable of understanding the problem was focused on the spaceship with the ultimatum delivered by its occupants. *Talk or Die!* blared the newspaper headlines.

The suicide rate was up and still climbing. Religious cults were having a field day. A book by a science fiction author, "What the Deadly Inter-Galactic Spaceship Means to You!", had smashed all previous best-seller records. And this had been going on for a frantic seven months.

The ship had *flapped* out of a gun-metal sky over Oregon, its shape that of a hideously magnified paramecium with edges that rippled like a mythological flying carpet. Its five green-skinned, frog-like occupants had delivered the ultimatum, one copy printed on velvety paper to each major government, each copy couched faultlessly in the appropriate native tongue:

"You are requested to assemble your most gifted experts in human communication. We are about to submit a problem. We will open five identical rooms of our vessel to you. One of us will be available in each room.

"Your problem: To communicate with us.

"If you succeed, your rewards will be great.

"If you fail, that will result in destruction for all sentient life on your planet.

"We announce this threat with the deepest regret. You are urged to examine Eniwetok atoll for a small display of our power. Your artificial satellites have been removed from the skies.

"You must break away from this limited communication!"

Eniwetok had been cleared off flat as a table at one thousand feet depth . . . with no trace of explosion! All

Russian and United States artificial satellites had been combed from the skies.

All day long a damp wind poured up the Columbia Gorge from the ocean. It swept across the Eastern Oregon alkali flats with a false prediction of rain. Spiny desert scrub bent before the gusts, sheltering blur-footed coveys of quail and flop-eared jackrabbits. Heaps of tumbleweed tangled in the fence lines, and the air was filled with dry particles of grit that crept under everything and into everything and on to everything with the omnipresence of filterable virus.

On the flats south of the Hermiston Ordnance Depot the weird bulk of the spaceship caught pockets and eddies of sand. The thing looked like a monstrous oval of dun canvas draped across upright sticks. A cluster of quonsets and the Army's new desert prefabs dotted a rough half-circle around the north rim. They looked like dwarfed out-buildings for the most gigantic circus tent Earth had ever seen. Army Engineers said the ship was six thousand two hundred and eighteen feet long, one thousand and fifty-four feet wide.

Some five miles east of the site the dust storm hazed across the monotonous structures of the cantonment that housed some thirty thousand people from every major nation: linguists, anthropologists, psychologists, doctors of every shape and description, watchers and watchers for the watchers, spies, espionage and counter-espionage agents.

For seven months the threat of Eniwetok, the threat of the unknown as well, had held them in check.

Towards evening of this day the wind slackened. The drifted sand began sifting off the ship and back into new shapes, trickling down for all the world like the figurative "sands of time" that here were most certainly running out.

Mrs Francine Millar, clinical psychologist with the Indo-European Germanic-Root team, hurried across the bare patch of trampled sand outside the spaceship's entrance. She bent her head against what was left of the windstorm. Under her left arm she carried her briefcase tucked up like a football. Her other hand carried a rolled-up copy of that afternoon's *Oregon Journal*. The lead story said that Air Force jets had shot down a small private plane trying to sneak into the restricted area. Three unidentified men killed. The plane had been stolen.

Thoughts of a plane crash made her too aware of the circumstances in her own recent widowhood. Dr Robert Millar had died in the crash of a transatlantic passenger plane ten days before the arrival of the spaceship. She let the newspaper fall out of her hands. It fluttered away on the wind.

Francine turned her head away from a sudden biting of the sandblast wind. She was a wiry slim figure of about five feet six inches, still trim and athletic at forty-one. Her auburn hair, mussed by the wind, still carried the look of youth. Heavy lids shielded her blue eyes. The lids drooped slightly, giving her a perpetual sleepy look even when she was wide awake and alert—a circumstance she found helpful in her profession.

She came into the lee of the conference quonset, and straightened. A layer of sand covered the doorstep. She opened the door, stepped across the sand only to find more of it on the floor inside, grinding underfoot. It was on tables, on chairs, mounded in corners—on every surface.

Hikonojo Ohashi, Francine's opposite number with the Japanese-Korean and Sino-Tibetan team, already sat at his place on the other side of the table. The Japanese psychologist was grasping, pen fashion, a thin pointed brush, making notes in ideographic shorthand.

Francine closed the door.

Ohashi spoke without looking up: "We're early."

He was a trim, neat little man: flat features, smooth cheeks, and even curve of chin, remote dark eyes behind the inevitable thick lenses of the Oriental scholar.

Francine tossed her briefcase on to the table, and pulled out a chair opposite Ohashi, She wiped away the grit with a handkerchief before sitting down. The ever present dirt, the monotonous landscape, her own frustration—all combined to hold her on the edge of anger. She recognized the feeling and its source, stifled a wry smile.

"No, Hiko," she said. "I think we're late. It's later than we think."

"Much later when you put it that way," said Ohashi. His Princeton accent came out low, modulated like a musical instrument under the control of a master.

"Now we're going to be banal," she said. Immediately, she regretted the sharpness of her tone, forced a smile to her lips.

"They gave us no deadline," said Ohashi. "That is one thing anyway." He twirled his brush across an inkstone.

"Something's in the air," she said. "I can feel it."

"Very much sand in the air," he said.

"You know what I mean," she said.

"The wind has us all on edge," he said. "It feels like rain. A change in the weather." He made another note, put down the brush, and began setting out papers for the conference. All at once, his head came up. He smiled at Francine. The smile made him look immature, and she suddenly saw back through the years to a serious little boy named Hiko Ohashi.

"It's been seven months," she said. "It stands to reason that they're not going to wait forever."

"The usual gestation period is two months longer," he said.

She frowned, ignoring the quip. "But we're no closer today than we were at the beginning!"

Ohashi leaned forward. His eyes appeared to swell behind the thick lenses. "Do you often wonder at their insistence that *we* communicate with *them*? I mean, rather than the other way around?"

"Of course I do. So does everybody else."

He sat back. "What do you think of the Islamic team's approach?"

"You know what I think, Hiko. It's a waste of time to compare all the Galactics' speech sounds to passages from the Koran." She shrugged. "But for all we know actually they could be closer to a solution than anyone else in . . ."

The door behind her banged open. Immediately, the room rumbled with the great basso voice of Theodore Zakheim, psychologist with the Ural-Altaic team.

"Hah-haaaaaaa!" he roared. "We're all here now!"

Light footsteps behind Zakheim told Francine that he was accompanied by Emile Goré of the Indo-European Latin-Root team.

Zakheim flopped on to a chair beside Francine. It creaked dangerously to his bulk.

Like a great uncouth bear! she thought.

"Do you always have to be so noisy?" she asked.

Goré slammed the door behind them.

"Naturally!" boomed Zakheim. "I am noisy! It's my nature, my little puchkin!"

Goré moved behind Francine, passing to the head of the table, but she kept her attention on Zakheim. He was a thick-bodied man, thick without fat, like the heaviness of a wrestler. His wide face and slanting pale blue eyes carried hints of Mongol ancestry. Rusty hair formed an uncombed brush atop his head.

Zakheim brought up his briefcase, flopped it on to the table, rested his hands on the dark leather. They were flat slab hands with thick fingers, pale wisps of hair growing down almost to the nails.

She tore her attention away from Zakheim's hands, looked down the table to where Goré sat. The Frenchman was a tall, gawk-necked man, entirely bald. Jet eyes behind steel-rimmed bifocals gave him a look of down-nose asperity like a comic bird. He wore one of his usual funereal black suits, every button secured. Knob wrists protruded from the sleeves. His long-fingered hands with their thick joints moved in constant restlessness.

"If I may differ with you, Zak," said Goré, "we are *not* all here. This is our same old group, and we were going to try to interest others in what we do here."

Ohashi spoke to Francine: "Have you had any luck inviting others to our conferences?"

"You can see that I'm alone," she said. "I chalked up five flat refusals today."

"Who?" asked Zakheim.

"The American Indian-Eskimo, the Hyperboreans, the Dravidians, the Malayo-Polynesians and the Caucasians."

"Hagglers!" barked Zakheim. "I, of course, can cover us with the Hamito-Semitic tongues, but . . ." He shook his head.

Goré turned to Ohashi. "The others?"

Ohashi said: "I must report the polite indifference of the Munda and Mon-Kmer, the Sudanese-Guinean and the Bantu."

"Those are big holes in our information exchange," said Goré. "What are they discovering?"

"No more than we are!" snapped Zakheim. "Depend on it!"

"What of the languages not even represented among the teams here on the international site?" asked Francine. "I mean the Hottentot-Bushmen, the Ainu, the Basque and the Australian-Papuan?"

Zakheim covered her left hand with his right hand. "You always have me, my little dove."

"We're building another Tower of Babel!" she snapped. She jerked her hand away.

"Spurned again," mourned Zakheim.

Ohashi said: "*Go to, let us go down, and there confound their language, that they may not understand one another's speech.*" He smiled. "Genesis eleven-seven."

Francine scowled. "And we're missing about twenty per cent of Earth's twenty-eight hundred languages!"

"We have all the significant ones," said Zakheim.

"How do *you* know what's significant?" she demanded.

"Please!" Goré raised a hand. "We're here to exchange information, not to squabble!"

"I'm sorry," said Francine. "It's just that I feel so hopeless today."

"Well, what have we learned today?" asked Goré.

"Nothing new with us," said Zakheim.

Goré cleared his throat. "That goes double for me." He looked at Ohashi.

The Japanese shrugged. "We achieved no reaction from the Galactic, Kobai."

"Anthropomorphic nonsense," muttered Zakheim.

"You mean naming him Kobai?" asked Ohashi. "Not at all, Zak. That's the most frequent sound he makes, and the name helps with identification. We don't have to keep referring to him as 'The Galactic' or 'that creature in the spaceship'."

Goré turned to Francine. "It was like talking to a green statue," she said.

"What of the lecture period?" asked Goré.

"Who knows?" she asked. "It stands there like a bow-legged professor in that black leotard. Those sounds spew out of it as though they'd never stop. It wriggles at us. It waves. It sways. Its face contorts, if you can call it a face. We recorded and filmed it all, naturally, but it sounded like the usual mish-mash!"

"There's something in the gestures," said Ohashi. "If we only had more competent pasimologists."

"How many times have you seen the same total gesture repeated with the same sound?" demanded Zakheim.

"You've carefully studied our films," said Ohashi. "Not enough times to give us a solid base for comparison. But I do not despair—"

"It was a rhetorical question," said Zakheim.

"We really need more multilinguists," said Goré. "Now is when we most miss the loss of such great linguists as Mrs Millar's husband."

Francine closed her eyes, took a short, painful breath. "Bob . . ." She shook her head. *No. That's the past. He's gone. The tears are ended.*

"I had the pleasure of meeting him in Paris shortly before the . . . end," continued Goré. "He was lecturing on the development of the similar sound schemes in Italian and Japanese."

Francine nodded. She felt suddenly empty.

Ohashi leaned forward. "I imagine this is . . . rather painful for Dr Millar," he said.

"I am *very* sorry," said Goré. "Forgive me."

"Someone was going to check and see if there are any electronic listening devices in this room," said Ohashi.

"My nephew is with our recording section," said Goré, "He assures me there are no hidden microphones here."

Zakheim's brows drew down into a heavy frown. He fumbled with the clasp of his briefcase. "This is very dangerous," he grunted.

"Oh, Zak, you always say that!" said Francine. "Let's quit playing footsy!"

"I do not enjoy the thought of treason charges," muttered Zakheim.

"We all know our bosses are looking for an advantage," she said. "I'm tired of these sparring matches where we each try to get something from the others without giving anything away!"

"If your Dr Langsmith or General Speidel found out what you were doing here, it would go hard for you, too," said Zakheim.

"I propose we take it from the beginning and re-examine everything," said Francine. "Openly this time."

"Why?" demanded Zakheim.

"Because I'm satisfied that the answer's right in front of us somewhere," she said.

"In the ultimatum, no doubt," said Goré. "What do you suppose is the *real* meaning of their statement that human languages are '*limited*' communication? Perhaps they are telepathic?"

"I don't think so," said Ohashi.

"That's pretty well ruled out," said Francine. "Our Rhine people say no ESP. No. I'm banking on something else: by the very fact that they posed this question, they have indicated that we *can* answer it with our present faculties."

"*If* they are being honest," said Zakheim.

"I have no recourse but to assume that they're honest," she said. "They're turning us into linguistic detectives for a good reason."

"A good reason for *them*," said Goré.

"Note the phraseology of their ultimatum," said Ohashi. "They *submit* a problem. They *open* their rooms to us. They are *available* to us. They *regret* their threat. Even their display of power—admittedly awe-inspiring—has the significant characteristic of non-violence. No explosion. They offer rewards for success, and this . . ."

"Rewards!" snorted Zakheim. "We lead the hog to its slaughter with a promise of food!"

"I suggest that they give evidence of being non-violent," said Ohashi. "Either that, or they have cleverly arranged themselves to present the *face* of non-violence."

Francine turned, and looked out of the hut's end window at the bulk of the spaceship. The low sun cast elongated shadows of the ship across the sand.

Zakheim, too, looked out of the window. "Why did they choose this place? If it had to be a desert, why not the Gobi? This is not even a good desert! This is a miserable desert!"

"Probably the easiest landing curve to a site near a large city," said Goré. "It is possible they chose a desert to avoid destroying arable land."

"Frogs!" snapped Zakheim. "I do not trust these frogs with their problem of communication!"

Francine turned back to the table, and took a pencil and scratch-pad from her briefcase. Briefly she sketched a rough outline of a Galactic, and wrote "frog?" beside it.

Ohashi said: "Are you drawing a picture of your Galactic?"

"We call it 'Uru' for the same reason you call yours 'Kobai'," she said. "It makes the sound 'Uru' ad nauseam."

She stared at her own sketch thoughtfully, calling up the memory image of the Galactic as she did so. Squat, about five feet ten inches in height, with the short bowed legs of a swimmer. Rippling muscles sent corded lines under the black leotard. The arms were articulated like a human's, but they were more graceful in movement. The skin was pale green, the neck thick and short. The wide mouth was almost lipless, the nose a mere blunt horn. The eyes were large and spaced wide with nictating lids. No hair, but a high crowned ridge from the centre of the forehead swept back across the head.

"I knew a Hawaiian distance swimmer once who looked much like these Galactics," said Ohashi. He wet his lips with his tongue. "You know, today we had a Buddhist monk from Java at our meeting with Kobai."

"I fail to see the association between a distance swimmer and a monk," said Goré.

"You told us you drew a blank today," said Zakheim.

"The monk tried no conversing," said Ohashi. "He refused because that would be a form of Earthly striving unthinkable for a Buddhist. He merely came and observed."

Francine leaned forward. "Yes?" She found an odd excitement in the way Ohashi was forcing himself to casualness.

"The monk's reaction was curious," said Ohashi. "He refused to speak for several hours afterwards. Then he said that these Galactics must be very holy people."

"Holy!" Zakheim's voice was edged with bitter irony.

"We are approaching this the wrong way," said Francine. She felt let down, spoke with a conscious effort. "Our access to these Galactics is limited by the space they've opened to us within their vessel."

"What is in the rest of the ship?" asked Zakheim.

"Rewards, perhaps," said Goré.

"Or weapons to demolish us!" snapped Zakheim.

"The pattern of the sessions is wrong too," said Francine.

Ohashi nodded. "Twelve hours a day is not enough," he said. "We should have them under constant observation."

"I didn't mean that," said Francine. "They probably

need rest just as we do. No. I meant the absolute control our team leaders—unimaginative men like Langsmith—have over the way we use our time in those rooms. For instance, what would happen if we tried to break down the force wall or whatever it is that keeps us from actually touching these creatures? What would happen if we brought in dogs to check how *animals* would react to them?" She reached in her briefcase, brought out a small flat recorder, and adjusted it for playback. "Listen to this."

There was a fluid burst of sound: "Pau'timónsh'uego' ikloprépre 'sauta' urusa'a'a . . ." and a long pause followed by: "tu'kimóomo 'urulig 'lurulil 'oog 'shuquetoé . . ." pause "sum 'a 'suma 'a 'uru 't 'shóap!'

Francine stopped the playback.

"Did you record that today?" asked Ohashi.

"Yes. It was using that odd illustration board with the moving pictures—weird flowers and weirder animals."

"We've seen them," muttered Zakheim.

"And those chopping movements of its hands," said Francine. "The swaying body, the undulations, the facial contortions." She shook her head. "It's almost like a bizarre dance."

"What are you driving at?" asked Ohashi.

"I've been wondering what would happen if we had a leading choreographer compose a dance to those sounds, and if we put it on for . . ."

"Faaa!" snorted Zakheim.

"All right," said Francine. "But we should be using some kind of random stimulation pattern on these Galactics. Why don't we bring in a nightclub singer? Or a circus barker? Or a magician? Or . . ."

"We tried a full-blown schizoid," said Goré.

Zakheim grunted. "And you got exactly what such tactics deserve: your schizoid sat there and played with his fingers for an hour!"

"The idea of using artists from the entertainment world intrigues me," said Ohashi. "Some *No* dancers, perhaps."

He nodded. "I'd never thought about it. But art is, after all, a form of communication."

"So is the croaking of a frog in a swamp," said Zakheim.

"Did you ever hear about the Paradox Frog?" asked Francine.

"Is this one of your strange jokes?" asked Zakheim.

"Of course not. The Paradox Frog is a very real creature. It lives on the island of Trinidad. It's a very small frog, but it has the opposable thumb on a five-fingered hand, and it . . ."

"Just like our visitors," said Zakheim.

"Yes. And it uses its hand just like we do—to grasp things, to pick up food, to stuff its mouth, to . . ."

"To make bombs?" asked Zakheim.

Francine shrugged, turned away. She felt hurt.

"My people believe these Galactics are putting on an elaborate sham," said Zakheim. "We think they are stalling while they secretly study us in preparation for invasion!"

Goré said: "So?" His narrow shoulders came up in a Gallic shrug that said as plainly as words: *"Even if this is true, what is there for us to do?"*

Francine turned to Ohashi. "What's the favourite theory current with your team?" Her voice sounded bitter, but she was unable to soften the tone.

"We are working on the assumption that this is a language of one-syllable root, as in Chinese," said Ohashi.

"But what of the vowel harmony?" protested Goré. "Surely that must mean the harmonious vowels are all in the same words."

Ohashi adjusted the set of his glasses. "Who knows?" he asked. "Certainly, the back vowels and front vowels come together many times, but . . ." He shrugged, shook his head.

"What's happening with the group that's working on the historical analogy?" asked Goré. "You were going to find out, Ohashi."

"They are working on the assumption that all primitive sounds are consonants with non-fixed vowels . . . footstampers for dancing, you know. Their current guess is that the Galactics are missionaries, their language a religious language."

"What results?" asked Zakheim.

"None."

Zakheim nodded. "To be expected." He glanced at Francine. "I beg the forgiveness of the Mrs Doctor Millar?"

She looked up, startled from a daydreaming speculation about the Galactic language and dancing. "Me? Good heavens, why?"

"I have been short-tempered today," said Zakheim. He glanced at his wristwatch. "I'm very sorry. I've been worried about another appointment."

He heaved his bulk out of the chair, took up his briefcase. "And it is time for me to be leaving. You forgive me?"

"Of course, Zak."

His wide face split into a grin. "Good!"

Goré got to his feet. "I will walk a little way with you, Zak."

Francine and Ohashi sat on for a moment after the others had gone.

"What good are we doing with these meetings?" she asked.

"Who knows how the important pieces of this puzzle will be fitted together?" asked Ohashi. "The point is: we are doing something different."

She sighed. "I guess so."

Ohashi took off his glasses, and it made him appear suddenly defenceless. "Did you know that Zak was recording our meeting?" he asked. He replaced the glasses.

Francine stared at him. "How do you know?"

Ohashi tapped his briefcase. "I have a device in here that reveals such things."

She swallowed a brief surge of anger. "Well, is it really important, Hiko?"

"Perhaps not." Ohashi took a deep, evenly controlled

breath. "I did not tell you one other thing about the Buddhist monk."

"Oh? What did you omit?"

"He predicts that we will fail—that the human race will be destroyed. He is very old and very cynical for a monk. He thinks it is a good thing that all human striving must eventually come to an end."

Anger and a sudden resolve flamed in her. "I don't care! I don't care what anyone else thinks! I know that . . ." She allowed her voice to trail off, put her hands to her eyes.

"You have been very distracted today," said Ohashi. "Did the talk about your late husband disturb you?"

"I know. I'm . . ." She swallowed, whispered: "I had a dream about Bob last night. We were dancing, and he was trying to tell me something about this problem, only I couldn't hear him. Each time he started to speak the music got louder and drowned him out."

Silence fell over the room. Presently, Ohashi said: "The unconscious mind takes strange ways sometimes to tell us the right answers. Perhaps we should investigate this idea of dancing."

"Oh, Hiko! Would you help me?"

"I should consider it an honour to help you," he said.

It was quiet in the semi-darkness of the projection room. Francine leaned her head against the back-rest of her chair, looked across at the stand light where Ohashi had been working. He had gone for the films on Oriental ritual dances that had just arrived from Los Angeles by plane. His coat was still draped across the back of his chair, his pipe still smouldered in the ashtray on the worktable. All around their two chairs were stacked the residue of four days' almost continuous research: notebooks, film cans, boxes of photographs, reference books.

She thought about Hiko Ohashi: a strange man. He was fifty and didn't look a day over thirty. He had grown children. His wife had died of cholera eight years ago. Francine wondered what it would be like married to an

Oriental, and she found herself thinking that he wasn't really Oriental with his Princeton education and Occidental ways. Then she realized that this attitude was a kind of white snobbery.

The door in the corner of the room opened softly. Ohashi came in, closed the door. "You awake?" he whispered.

She turned her head without lifting it from the chairback. "Yes."

"I'd hoped you might fall asleep for a bit," he said. "You looked so tired when I left."

Francine glanced at her wristwatch. "It's only three-thirty. What's the day like?"

"Hot and windy."

Ohashi busied himself inserting film into the projector at the rear of the room. Presently, he went to his chair, trailing the remote control cable for the projector.

"Ready?" he asked.

Francine reached for the low editing light beside her chair, and turned it on, focusing the narrow beam on a notebook in her lap. "Yes. Go ahead."

"I feel that we're making real progress," said Ohashi. "It's not clear yet, but the points of identity . . ."

"They're exciting," she said. "Let's see what this one has to offer."

Ohashi punched the button on the cable. A heavily robed Arab girl appeared on the screen, slapping a tambourine. Her hair looked stiff, black and oily. A sooty line of kohl shaded each eye. Her brown dress swayed slightly as she tinkled the tambourine, then slapped it.

The cultured voice of the commentator came through the speaker beside the screen: "This is a young girl of Jebel Tobeyk. She is going to dance some very ancient steps that tell a story of battle. The camera is hidden in a truck, and she is unaware that this dance is being photographed."

A reed flute joined the tambourine, and a twanging stringed instrument came in behind it. The girl turned slowly on one foot, the other raised with knee bent.

Francine watched in rapt silence. The dancing girl made short staccato hops, the tambourine jerking in front of her.

"It is reminiscent of some of the material on the Norse sagas," said Ohashi. "Battle with swords. Note the thrust and parry."

She nodded. "Yes." The dance stamped onward, then: "Wait! Re-run that last section."

Ohashi obeyed.

It started with a symbolic trek on camel-back: swaying, undulating. The dancing girl expressed longing for her warrior. *How suggestive the motions of her hands along her hips,* thought Francine. With a feeling of abrupt shock, she recalled seeing almost the exact gesture from one of the films of the Galactics. "There's one!" she cried.

"The hands on the hips," said Ohashi. "I was just about to stop the reel." He shut off the film, searched through the notebooks around him until he found the correct reference.

"I think it was one of Zak's films," said Francine.

"Yes. Here it is." Ohashi brought up a reel, looked at the scene identifications. He placed the film can on a large stack behind him, re-started the film of Oriental dances.

Three hours and ten minutes later they put the film back in its can.

"How many new comparisons do you make it?" asked Ohashi.

"Five," she said. "That makes one hundred and six in all!" Francine leafed through her notes. "There was the motion of the hands on the hips. I call that one sensual pleasure."

Ohashi lighted a pipe, spoke through a cloud of smoke. "The others: how have you labelled them?"

"Well, I've just put a note on the motions of one of the Galactics and then the commentator's remarks from this dance film. Chopping motion of the hand ties to the end of Sobàya's first dream: *'Now, I awaken!'* Undulation of the body ties in with swaying of date palms in the desert wind. Stamping of the foot goes with Torak dismounting from his steed. Lifting hands, palms up—that goes with Ali offering his soul to God in prayer before battle."

"Do you want to see this latest film from the ship?" asked Ohashi. He glanced at his wristwatch. "Or shall we get a bite to eat first?"

She waved a hand distractedly. "The film. I'm not hungry. The film." She looked up. "I keep feeling that there's something I should remember . . . something . . ." She shook her head.

"Think about it a few minutes," said Ohashi. "I'm going to send out these other films to be cut and edited according to our selections. And I'll have some sandwiches sent in while I'm at it."

Francine rubbed at her forehead. "All right."

Ohashi gathered up a stack of film cans, left the room. He knocked out his pipe on a "No Smoking" sign beside the door as he left.

"Consonants," whispered Francine. "The ancient alphabets were almost exclusively made up of consonants. Vowels came later. They were the softeners, the swayers." She chewed at her lower lip. "Language constricts the *ways* you can think." She rubbed at her forehead. "Oh, if I only had Bob's ability with languages!"

She tapped her fingers on the chair arm. "It has something to do with our emphasis on *things* rather than on people and the things people do. Every Indo-European language is the same on that score. If only . . ."

"Talking to yourself?" It was a masculine voice, startling her because she had not heard the door open.

Francine jerked upright, turned towards the door. Dr Irving Langsmith, chief of the American Division of the Germanic-Root team, stood just inside, closing the door.

"Haven't seen you for a couple of days," he said. "We got your note that you were indisposed." He looked around the room, then at the clutter on the floor beside the chairs.

Francine blushed.

Dr Langsmith crossed to the chair Ohashi had occupied,

sat down. He was a grey-haired runt of a man with a heavily seamed face, small features—a gnome figure with hard eyes. He had the reputation of an organizer and politician with more drive than genius. He pulled a stubby pipe from his pocket, lighted it.

"I probably should have cleared this through channels," she said. "But I had visions of it getting bogged down in red tape, especially with Hiko . . . I mean with another team represented in this project."

"Quite all right," said Langsmith. "We knew what you were up to within a couple of hours. Now, we want to know what you've discovered. Dr Ohashi looked pretty excited when he left here a bit ago."

Her eyes brightened. "I think we're on to something," she said. "We've compared the Galactics' movements to known symbolism from primitive dances."

Dr Langsmith chuckled. "That's very interesting, my dear, but surely you . . ."

"No, really!" she said. "We've found one hundred and six points of comparison, almost exact duplication of movements!"

"Dances? Are you trying to tell me that . . ."

"I know it sounds strange," she said, "but we . . ."

"Even if you *have* found exact points of comparison, that means nothing," said Langsmith. "These are *aliens* . . . from another world. You've no right to assume that their language development would follow the same pattern as ours has."

"But they're humanoid!" she said. "Don't you believe that language started as the unconscious shaping of the *speech* organs to imitate *bodily* gestures?"

"It's highly likely," said Langsmith.

"We can make quite a few pretty safe assumptions about them," she said. "For one thing, they apparently have a rather high standard of civilization to be able to construct—"

"Let's not labour the obvious," interrupted Langsmith, a little impatiently.

Francine studied the team chief a moment, said: "Did you ever hear how Marshal Foch planned his military campaigns?"

Langsmith puffed on his pipe, took it out of his mouth. "Uh . . . are you suggesting that a military . . ."

"He wrote out the elements of his problem on a sheet of paper," said Francine. "At the top of the paper went the lowest common denominator. There, he wrote: *'Problem—To beat the Germans.'* Quite simple. Quite obvious. But oddly enough *beating the enemy* has frequently been overlooked by commanders who got too involved in complicated manoeuvres."

"Are you suggesting that the Galactics are enemies?"

She shook her head indignantly. "I am *not*! I'm suggesting that language is primarily an instinctive social reflex. The least common denominator of a social problem is a human being. One single human being. And here we are all involved with getting this thing into mathematical equations and neat word frequency primarily oral!"

"But you've been researching a visual . . ."

"Yes! But only as it modifies the sounds." She leaned towards Langsmith. "Dr Langsmith, I believe that this language is a *flexional* language with the flexional endings and root changes contained entirely in the bodily movements!"

"Hmmmmmmmm." Langsmith studied the smoke spiralling ceilingwards from his pipe. "Fascinating idea!"

"We can assume that this is a highly standardized language," said Francine. "Basing the assumption on their high standard of civilization. The two usually go hand in hand."

Langsmith nodded.

"Then the gestures, the sounds would tend to be ritual," she said.

"Mmmmm-hmmmm."

"Then . . . may we have the help to go into this idea the way it deserves?" she asked.

"I'll take it up at the next top staff meeting," said Langsmith. He got to his feet. "Don't get your hopes up. This'll have to be submitted to the electronic computers. It probably has been cross-checked and rejected in some other problem."

She looked up at him, dismayed. "But . . . Dr Langsmith . . . a computer's no better than what's put into it. I'm certain that we're stepping out into a region here where we'll have to build up a whole new approach to language."

"Now, don't you worry, said Langsmith. He frowned. "No . . . don't worry about *this*."

"Shall we go ahead with what we're doing then?" she asked. "I mean—do we have permission to?"

"Yes, yes . . . of course." Langsmith wiped his mouth with the back of his hand. "General Speidel has called a special meeting tomorrow morning. I'd like to have you attend. I'll send somebody to pick you up." He waved a hand at the litter around Francine. "Carry on, now." There was a pathetic emptiness to the way he put his pipe in his mouth and left the room. Francine stared at the closed door.

She felt herself trembling, and recognized that she was deathly afraid. *Why?* she asked herself. *What have I sensed to make me afraid?*

Presently, Ohashi came in carrying a paper bag.

"Saw Langsmith going out," he said. "What did he want?"

"He wanted to know what we're doing."

Ohashi paused beside his chair. "Did you tell him?"

"Yes. I asked for help." She shook her head. "He wouldn't commit himself."

"I brought ham sandwiches," said Ohashi.

Francine's chin lifted abruptly. "Defeated!" she said. "That's it! He acted completely defeated!"

"What?"

"I've been trying to puzzle through the strange way Langsmith was acting. He just radiated defeat."

Ohashi handed her a sandwich. "Better brace yourself for a shock," he said. "I ran into Tsu Ong, liaison officer for our delegation . . . in the cafeteria." The Japanese raised the sandwich sack over his chair, dropped it into the seat with a curious air of preciseness. "The Russians are pressing for a combined attack on the Galactic ship to wrest their secret from them by force."

Francine buried her face in her hands. "The fools!" she whispered. "Oh, the fools!" Abruptly, sobs shook her. She found herself crying with the same uncontrollable racking that had possessed her when she'd learned of her husband's death.

Ohashi waited silently.

The tears subsided. Control returned. She swallowed, said: "I'm sorry."

"Do not be sorry." He put a hand on her shoulder. "Shall we knock off for the night?"

She put her hand over his, shook her head. "No. Let's look at the latest films from the ship."

"As you wish." Ohashi pulled away, threaded a new film into the projector.

Presently, the screen came alive to a blue-grey alcove filled with pale light: one of the "class" rooms in the spaceship. A squat, green-skinned figure stood in the centre of the room. Beside the Galactic was the pedestal-footed projection board that all five used to illustrate their "lectures". The board displayed a scene of a wide blue lake, reeds along the shore stirring to a breeze.

The Galactic swayed. His face moved like a ripple of water. He said: "Ahon'atu'uklah'shoginai' eástruru." The green arms moved up and down, undulating. The webbed hands came out, palms facing and almost touching, began chopping from the wrists: up, down, up, down, up, down . . .

On the projection board the scene switched to an under-water view: myriad swimming shapes coming closer, closer—large-eyed fish creatures with long ridged tails.

"Five will get you ten," said Ohashi. "Those are the young of this Galactic race. Notice the ridge."

"Tadpoles," said Francine.

The swimming shapes darted through orange shadows and into a space of cold green—then up to splash on the surface, and again down into the cool green. It was a choreographic swinging, lifting, dipping, swaying—lovely in its synchronized symmetry.

"Chiruru'uklia'a'agudav'iaá," said the Galactic. His body undulated like the movements of the swimming creatures. The green hands touched his thighs, slipped upward until elbows were level with shoulders.

"The maiden in the Oriental dance," said Francine.

Now, the hands came out, palms up, in a gesture curiously suggestive of giving. The Galactic said: "Pluainumiuri!" in a single burst of sound that fell on their ears like an explosion.

"It's like a distorted version of the ritual dances we've been watching," said Ohashi.

"I've a hunch," said Francine. "Feminine intuition. The repeated vowels: they could be an adverbial emphasis, like our word *very*. Where it says '*a-a-a*' note the more intense gestures."

She followed another passage, nodding her head to the gestures. "Hiko, could this be a constructed language? Artificial?"

"The thought has occurred to me," said Ohashi.

Abruptly, the projector light dimmed, the action slowed. All lights went out. They heard a dull, booming roar in the distance, a staccato rattling of shots. Feet pounded along the corridor outside the room.

Francine sat in stunned silence.

Ohashi said: "Stay here, please. I will have a look around to see what . . ."

The door banged open and a flashlight beam stabbed into the room, momentarily blinding them.

"Everything all right in here?" boomed a masculine voice.

They made out a white MP helmet visible behind the light.

"Yes," said Ohashi. "What is happening?"

"Somebody blew up a tower to the main transmission line from McNary Dam. Then there was an attempt to breach our security blockade on the south. Everything will be back to normal shortly." The light turned away.

"Who?" asked Francine.

"Some crazy civilians," said the MP. "We'll have the emergency power on in a minute. Just stay in this room until we give the all clear." He left, closing the door.

They heard a rattle of machine-gun fire. Another explosion shook the building. Voices shouted.

"We are witnessing the end of a world," said Ohashi.

"Our world ended when that spaceship set down here," she said.

Abruptly, the lights came on: dimly, then brighter. The projector resumed its whirring. Ohashi turned it off.

Somebody walked down the corridor outside, rapped on the door, said: "All clear." The footsteps receded down the hall, and they heard another rapping, a fainter "All clear".

"Civilians," she said. "What do you suppose they wanted so desperately to do a thing like that?"

"They are a symptom of the general sickness," said Ohashi. "One way to remove a threat is to destroy it—even if you destroy yourself in the process. These civilians are only a minor symptom."

"The Russians are the big symptom then," she said.

"Every major government is a *big* symptom right now," he said.

"I . . . I think I'll get back to my room," she said. "Let's take up again tomorrow morning. Eight o'clock all right?"

"Quite agreeable," said Ohashi. "If there is a tomorrow."

"Don't *you* get that way, too," she said, and she took a quavering breath. "I refuse to give up."

Ohashi bowed. He was suddenly very Oriental. "There is a primitive saying of the Ainu," he said: *"The world ends every night . . . and begins anew every morning."*

It was a room dug far underground beneath the Ordnance

Depot, originally for storage of atomics. The walls were lead. It was an oblong space: about thirty by fifteen feet, with a very low ceiling. Two trestle tables had been butted end-to-end in the centre of the room to form a single long surface. A series of green-shaded lights suspended above this table gave the scene an odd resemblance to a gambling room. The effect was heightened by the set look to the shoulders of the men sitting in spring-bottom chairs around the table. There were a scattering of uniforms: Air Force, Army, Marines; plus hard-faced civilians in expensive suits.

Dr Langsmith occupied a space at the middle of one of the table's sides and directly across from the room's only door. His gnome features were locked in a frown of concentration. He puffed rhythmically at the stubby pipe like a witchman creating an oracle smoke.

A civilian across the table from Langsmith addressed a two-star general seated beside the team chief: "General Speidel, I still think this is too delicate a spot to risk a woman."

Speidel grunted. He was a thin man with a high, narrow face: an aristocratic face that radiated granite convictions and stubborn pride. There was an air about him of spring steel under tension and vibrating to a chord that dominated the room.

"Our choice is limited," said Langsmith. "Very few of our personnel have consistently taken wheeled carts into the ship *and* consistently taken a position close to that force barrier or whatever it is."

Speidel glanced at his wristwatch. "What's keeping them?"

"She may already have gone to breakfast," said Langsmith.

"Be better if we got her in here hungry and jumpy," said the civilian.

"Are you sure you can handle her, Smitty?" asked Speidel.

Langsmith took his pipe from his mouth, peered into the

stem as though the answer were to be found there. "We've got her pretty well analysed," he said. "She's a recent widow, you know. Bound to still have a rather active deathwish structure."

There was a buzzing of whispered conversation from a group of officers at one end of the table. Speidel tapped his fingers on the arm of his chair.

Presently, the door opened. Francine entered. A hand reached in from outside, closed the door behind her.

"Ah, there you are, Dr Millar," said Langsmith. He got to his feet. There was a scuffling sound around the table as the others arose. Langsmith pointed to an empty chair diagonally across from him. "Sit down, please."

Francine advanced into the light. She felt intimidated, knew she showed it, and the realization filled her with a feeling of bitterness tinged with angry resentment. The ride down the elevator from the surface had been an experience she never wanted to repeat. It had seemed many times longer than it actually was—like a descent into Dante's Inferno.

She nodded to Langsmith, glanced covertly at the others, took the indicated chair. It was a relief to get the weight off her trembling knees, and she momentarily relaxed, only to tense up again as the others resumed their seats. She put her hands on the table, immediately withdrew them to hold them clasped tightly in her lap.

"Why was I brought here like a prisoner?" she demanded.

Langsmith appeared honestly startled. "But I told you last night that I'd send somebody for you."

Speidel chuckled easily. "Some of our Security boys are a little grim-faced," he said. "I hope they didn't frighten you."

She took a deep breath, began to relax. "Is this about the request I made last night?" she asked. "I mean for help in this new line of research?"

"In a way," said Langsmith. "But first I'd like to have you answer a question for me." He pursed his lips. "Uh . . . I've never asked one of my people for just a wild guess before, but

I'm going to break that rule with you. What's your guess as to why these Galactics are here?"

"Guess?"

"Logical assumption, then," he said.

She looked down at her hands. "We've all speculated, of course. They might be scientists investigating us for reasons of their own."

"Damnation!" barked the civilian beside her. Then: "Sorry, ma'm. But that's the pap we keep using to pacify the public."

"And we aren't keeping them very well pacified," said Langsmith. "That group that stormed us last night called themselves the *Sons of Truth!* They had thermite bombs, and were going to attack the spaceship."

"How foolish," she whispered. "How pitiful."

"Go on with your guessing, Dr Millar," said Speidel.

She glanced at the general, again looked at her hands. "There's the military's idea—that they want Earth for a strategic base in some kind of space war."

"It could be," said Speidel.

"They could be looking for more living space for their own kind," she said.

"In which case, what happens to the native population?" asked Langsmith.

"They would either be exterminated or enslaved, I'm afraid. But the Galactics could be commercial traders of some sort, interested in our art forms, our animals for their zoos, our archaeology, our spices, our . . ." She broke off, shrugged. "How do we know what they may be doing on the side . . . secretly?"

"Exactly!" said Speidel. He glanced sidelong at Langsmith. "She talks pretty level-headed, Smitty."

"But I don't believe any of these things," she said.

"What is it you believe?" asked Speidel.

"I believe they're just what they represent themselves to be—representatives of a powerful Galactic culture that is immeasurably superior to our own."

"Powerful, all right!" It was a marine officer at the far end of the table. "The way they cleaned off Eniwetok and swept our satellites out of the skies!"

"Do you think there's a possibility they could be concealing their true motives?" asked Langsmith.

"A possibility, certainly."

"Have you ever watched a confidence man in action?" asked Langsmith.

"I don't believe so. But you're not seriously suggesting that these . . ." She shook her head. "Impossible."

"The *mark* seldom gets wise until it's too late," said Langsmith.

She looked puzzled. "Mark?"

"The fellow the confidence men choose for a victim." Langsmith re-lighted his pipe, extinguished the match by shaking it. "Dr Millar, we have a very painful disclosure to make to you."

She straightened, feeling a sudden icy chill in her veins at the stillness in the room.

"Your husband's death was not an accident," said Langsmith.

She gasped, and turned deathly pale.

"In the six months before this spaceship landed, there were some twenty-eight mysterious deaths," said Langsmith. "More than that, really, because innocent bystanders died, too. These accidents had a curious similarity: in each instance there was a fatality of a foremost expert in the field of language, cryptoanalysis, semantics . . ."

"The people who might have solved this problem died before the problem was even presented," said Speidel. "Don't you think that's a curious coincidence."

She was unable to speak.

"In one instance there was a survivor," said Langsmith. "A British jet transport crashed off Ceylon, killing Dr Ramphit U. The lone survivor, the co-pilot, said a brilliant beam of light came from the sky overhead and sliced off the port wing. Then it cut the cabin in half!"

Francine put a hand to her throat. Langsmith's cautious hand movements suddenly fascinated her.

"Twenty-eight air crashes?" she whispered.

"No. Two were auto crashes." Langsmith puffed a cloud of smoke before his face.

Her throat felt sore. She swallowed, said: "But how can you be sure of that?"

"It's circumstantial evidence, yes," said Speidel. He spoke with thin-lipped precision. "But there's more. For the past four months all astronomical activity of our nation has been focused on the near heavens, including the moon. Our attention was drawn to evidence of activity near the moon crater Theophilus. We have been able to make out the landing rockets of more than five hundred spacecraft!"

"What do you think of that?" asked Langsmith. He nodded behind his smoke screen.

She could only stare at him; her lips ashen.

"These *frogs* have massed an invasion fleet on the moon!" snapped Speidel. "It's obvious!"

They're lying to me! she thought. *Why this elaborate pretence?* She shook her head, and something her husband had once said leapt unbidden into her mind: *"Language clutches at us with unseen fingers. It conditions us to the way others are thinking. Through language, we impose upon each other our ways of looking at things."*

Speidel leaned forward. "We have more than a hundred atomic warheads aimed at that moon-base! One of those warheads will do the job if it gets through!" He hammered a fist on the table. "But first we have to capture this ship here!"

Why are they telling me all this? she asked herself. She drew in a ragged breath, said: "Are you sure you're right?"

"Of course we're sure!" Speidel leaned back, lowered his voice. "Why else would they insist we learn their language? The first thing a conqueror does is impose his language on his new slaves!"

"No . . . no, wait," she said. "That only applies to recent

history. You're getting language mixed up with patriotism because of our own imperial history. Bob always said that such misconceptions are a serious hindrance to sound historical scholarship."

"We know what we're talking about, Dr Millar," said Speidel.

"You're suspicious of language because our imperialism went hand in hand with our language," she said.

Speidel looked at Langsmith. "You talk to her."

"If there actually were communication in the sounds these Galactics make, you know we'd have found it by now," said Langsmith. "You know it!"

She spoke in sudden anger: "I don't know it! In fact, I feel that we're on the verge of solving their language with this new approach we've been working on."

"Oh, come now!" said Speidel. "Do you mean that after our finest cryptographers have worked over this thing for seven months, you disagree with them entirely?"

"No, no, let her say her piece," said Langsmith.

"We've tapped a new source of information in attacking this problem," she said. "Primitive dances."

"Dances?" Speidel looked shocked.

"Yes. I think the Galactics' gestures may be their adjectives and adverbs—the full emotional content of their language."

"Emotion!" snapped Speidel. "Emotion isn't language!"

She repressed a surge of anger, said: "We're dealing with something completely outside our previous experience. We have to discard old ideas. We know that the habits of a native tongue set up a person's speaking responses. In fact, you can define language as the system of habits you reveal when you speak."

Speidel tapped his fingers on the table, stared at the door behind Francine.

She ignored his nervous distraction, said: "The Galactics use almost the full range of implosive and glottal stops with a wide selection of vowel sounds: fricatives, plosives, voiced and unvoiced. And we note an apparent lack of the usual interfering habits you find in normal speech."

"This isn't normal speech!" blurted Speidel. "Those are nonsense sounds!" He shook his head. "Emotions!"

"All right," she said. "Emotions! We're pretty certain that language begins with emotions—pure emotional actions. The baby pushes away the plate of unwanted food."

"You're wasting our time!" barked Speidel.

"I didn't ask to come down here," she said.

"Please." Langsmith put a hand on Speidel's arm. "Let Dr Millar have her say."

"Emotion," muttered Speidel.

"Every spoken language of earth has migrated away from emotion," said Francine.

"Can you write an emotion on paper?" demanded Speidel.

"That does it," she said. "That really tears it! You're blind! You say language has to be written down. That's part of the magic! Your mind is tied in little knots by academic tradition! Language, General, is primarily oral! People like you, though, want to make it into ritual noise!"

"I didn't come down here for an egg-head argument!" snapped Speidel.

"Let me handle this, please," said Langsmith. He made a mollifying gesture towards Francine. "Please continue."

She took a deep breath. "I'm sorry I snapped," she said. She smiled. "I think we let emotion get the best of us."

Speidel frowned.

"I was talking about language moving away from emotion," she said. "Take Japanese, for example. Instead of saying, 'Thank you' they say, 'Katajikenai'—'I am insulted'. Or they say, 'Kino doku' which means 'This poisonous feeling!'" She held up her hands. "This is ritual exclusion of showing emotion. Our Indo-European languages—especially Anglo-Saxon tongues—are moving the same way. We seem to think that emotion isn't quite nice, that . . ."

"It tells you nothing!" barked Speidel.

She forced down the anger that threatened to overwhelm her. "If you can read the emotional signs," she said, "they reveal if a speaker is telling the truth. That's all, General. They just tell you if you're getting at the truth. Any good psychologist knows this, General. Freud said it: 'If you try to conceal your feelings, every pore oozes betrayal.' You seem to think that the opposite is true."

"Emotions! Dancing!" Speidel pushed his chair back. "Smitty, I've had as much of this as I can take."

"Just a minute," said Langsmith. "Now, Dr Millar, I wanted you to have your say because we've already considered these points. Long ago. You're interested in the gestures. You say this is a dance of emotions. Other experts say with equal emphasis that these gestures are ritual combat! Freud, indeed! They ooze betrayal. This chopping gesture they make with the right hand"—he chopped the air in illustration—"is identical to the karate or judo chop for breaking the human neck!"

Francine shook her head, put a hand to her throat. She was momentarily overcome by a feeling of uncertainty.

Langsmith said: "That outward thrust they make with one hand: that's the motion of a sword being shoved into an opponent! They ooze betrayal all right!"

She looked from Langsmith to Speidel, back to Langsmith. A man to her right cleared his throat.

Langsmith said: "I've just given you two examples. We have hundreds more. Every analysis we've made has come up with the same answer: treachery! The pattern's as old as time: offer a reward: pretend friendship; get the innocent lamb's attention on your empty hand while you poise the axe in your other hand!"

Could I be wrong? she wondered. *Have we been duped by these Galactics?* Her lips trembled. She fought to control them, whispered: "Why are you telling me these things?"

"Aren't you at all interested in revenge against the creatures who murdered your husband?" asked Speidel.

"I don't know that they murdered him!" She blinked back tears. "You're trying to confuse me!" And a favourite saying of her husband's came into her mind: *"A conference is a group of people making a difficult job out of what one person could do easily."* The room suddenly seemed too close and oppressive.

"Why have I been dragged into this conference?" she demanded. "Why?"

"We were hoping you'd assist us in capturing that spaceship," said Langsmith.

"Me? Assist you in . . ."

"Someone has to get a bomb past the force screens at the door—the ones that keep sand and dirt out of the ship. We've got to have a bomb inside."

"But why me?"

"They're used to seeing you wheel in the master recorder on that cart," said Langsmith. "We thought of putting a bomb in . . ."

"No!"

"This has gone far enough," said Speidel. He took a deep breath, started to rise.

"Wait," said Langsmith.

"She obviously has no feelings of patriotic responsibility," said Speidel. "We're wasting our time."

Langsmith said: "The Galactics are used to seeing her with that cart. If we change now, they're liable to become suspicious."

"We'll set up some other plan, then," said Speidel. "As far as I'm concerned, we can write off any possibility of further co-operation from her."

"You're little boys playing a game," said Francine. "This isn't an exclusive American problem. This is a human problem that involves every nation on Earth."

"That ship is on United States soil," said Speidel.

"Which happens to be on the only planet controlled by the human species," she said. "We ought to be sharing everything with the other teams, pooling information and ideas to get at every scrap of knowledge."

"We'd all like to be idealists," said Speidel. "But there's no room for idealism where our survival is concerned. These *frogs* have full space travel, apparently between the stars—not just satellites and moon rockets. If we get their ship we can enforce peace on our own terms."

"National survival," she said. "But it's our survival as a species that's at stake!"

Speidel turned to Langsmith. "This is one of your more spectacular failures, Smitty. We'll have to put her under close surveillance."

Langsmith puffed furiously on his pipe. A cloud of pale blue smoke screened his head. "I'm ashamed of you, Dr Millar," he said.

She jumped to her feet, allowing her anger full scope at last. "You must think I'm a rotten psychologist!" she snapped. "You've been lying to me since I set foot in here!" She shot a bitter glance at Speidel. "Your gestures gave you away! The non-communicative emotional gestures, General!"

"What's she talking about?" demanded Speidel.

"You said different things with your mouths than you said with your bodies," she explained. "That means you were lying to me—concealing something vital you didn't want me to know about."

"She's insane!" barked Speidel.

"There wasn't any survivor of a plane crash in Ceylon," she said. "There probably wasn't even the plane crash you described."

Speidel froze to sudden stillness, spoke through thin lips: "Has there been a security leak? Good Lord!"

"Look at Dr Langsmith there!" she said. "Hiding behind that pipe! And you, General: moving your mouth no more than absolutely necessary to speak—trying to hide your real feelings! Oozing betrayal!"

"Get her out of here!" barked Speidel.

"You're all logic and no intuition!" she shouted. "No understanding of feeling and art! Well, General: go back to your computers, but remember this—you can't build a machine that thinks like a man! You can't feed emotion into an electronic computer and get back anything except numbers! Logic, to you, General!"

"I said get her out of here!" shouted Speidel. He rose half out of his chair, turned to Langsmith who sat in pale silence. "And I want a thorough investigation! I want to know where the security leak was that put her wise to our plans."

"Watch yourself!" snapped Langsmith.

Speidel took two deep breaths, sank back.

They're insane, thought Francine. *Insane and pushed into a corner. With that kind of fragmentation they could slip into catatonia or violence.* She felt weak and afraid.

Others around the table had arisen. Two civilians moved up beside Francine. "Shall we lock her up, General?" asked one.

Speidel hesitated.

Langsmith spoke first: "No. Just keep her under very close surveillance. If we locked her up it would arouse questions that we don't want to answer."

Speidel glowered at Francine. "If you give us away, I'll have you shot!" He motioned to have her taken out of the room.

When she emerged from the headquarters building, Francine's mind still whirled. *Lies!* she thought. *All lies!*

She felt the omnipresent sand grate under her feet. Dust hazed the concourse between her position on the steps and the spaceship a hundred yards away. The morning sun already had burned off the night chill of the desert. Heat devils danced over the dun surface of the ship.

Francine ignored the security agent loitering a few steps behind her, glanced at her wristwatch: nine-twenty. *Hiko will be wondering what's happened to me,* she thought. *We were supposed to get started by eight.* Hopelessness gripped her mind. The spaceship looming over the end of the concourse appeared like a malignant growth—an evil thing crouched ready to envelope and smother her.

Could that fool general be right? The thought came to her mind unbidden. She shook her head. *No! He was lying! But why did he want me to . . .* Delayed realization broke off the thought. *They wanted me to take a small bomb inside the ship, but there was no mention of my escaping! I'd have had to stay with the cart and the bomb to allay suspicions. My God! Those beasts expected me to commit suicide for them! They wanted me to blame the Galactics for Bob's death! They tried to build a lie in my mind until I'd fall in with their plan. It's hard enough to die for an ideal, but to give up your life for a lie . . .*

Anger coursed through her. She stopped on the steps, stood there shivering. A new feeling of futility replaced the anger. Tears blurred her vision. *What can one lone woman do against such ruthless schemers?*

Through her tears, she saw movement on the concourse: a man in civilian clothes crossing from right to left. Her mind registered the movement with only partial awareness: *man stops, points.* She was suddenly alert, tears gone, following the direction of the civilian's extended right arm, hearing his voice shout: "Hey! Look at that!"

A thin needle of an aircraft stitched a hurtling line across the watery desert sky. It banked, arrowed towards the spaceship. Behind it roared an airforce jet—delta wings vibrating, sun flashing off polished metal. Tracers laced out towards the airship.

Someone's attacking the spaceship! she thought. *It's a Russian ICBM!*

But the needle braked abruptly, impossibly, over the spaceship. Behind it, the airforce jet's engine died, and there was only the eerie whistling of air burning across its wings.

Gently, the needle lowered itself into a fold of the spaceship.

It's one of theirs—the Galactics' she realized. *Why is it coming here now? Do they suspect attack? Is that some kind of reinforcement?*

Deprived of its power, the jet staggered, skimmed out to a dust-geyser, belly-landing in the alkali flats. Sirens screamed as emergency vehicles raced towards it.

The confused sounds gave Francine a sudden feeling of nausea. She took a deep breath, and stepped down to the concourse, moving without conscious determination, her thoughts in a turmoil. The grating sand beneath her feet was like an emery surface rubbing her nerves. She was acutely conscious of an acrid, burning odour, and she realized with a sudden stab of alarm that her security guard still waited behind her on the steps of the administration building.

Vaguely, she heard voices babbling in the building doorways on both sides of the concourse—people coming out to stare at the spaceship and off across the flats where red trucks clustered around the jet.

A pebble had worked its way into her right shoe. Her mind registered it, rejected an urge to stop and remove the irritant. An idea was trying to surface in her mind. Momentarily, she was distracted by a bee humming across her path. Quite inanely her mind dwelt on the thought that the insect was too commonplace for this moment. A mental drunkenness made her giddy. She felt both elated and terrified. *Danger! Yes: terrible danger*, she thought. *Obliteration for the entire human race. But something had to be done. She started to run.* . . .

An explosion rocked the concourse, threw her stumbling to her hands and knees. Sand burned against her palms. Dumb instinct brought her back to her feet. Another explosion—farther away to the right, behind the buildings. Bitter smoke swept across the concourse. Abruptly, men lurched from behind the buildings on the right, slogging through the sand towards the spaceship.

Civilians! Possibly—and yet they moved with the purposeful unity of soldiers.

It was like a dream scene to Francine. The men carried weapons. She stopped, saw the gleam of sunlight on metal, heard the peculiar crunch-crunch of men running in sand. Through a dreamy haze she recognized one of the runners: Zakheim. He carried a large black box on his shoulders. His red hair flamed out in the group like a target.

The Russians! she thought. *They've started their attack! If our people join them now, it's the end!*

A machine-gun stuttered somewhere to her right. Dust puffs walked across the concourse, swept into the running figures. Men collapsed, but others still slogged towards the spaceship. An explosion lifted the leaders, sent them sprawling. Again, the machine-gun chattered. Dark figures lay on the sand like thrown dominoes. But still a few continued their mad charge.

MPs in American uniforms ran out from between the buildings on the right. The leaders carried submachine-guns.

We're stopping the attack, thought Francine. But she knew the change of tactics did not mean a rejection of violence by Speidel and the others. It was only a move to keep the Russians from taking the lead. She clenched her fists, ignored the fact that she stood exposed—a lone figure in the middle of the concourse. Her senses registered an eerie feeling of unreality.

Machine-guns renewed their chatter and then—abrupt silence. But now the last of the Russians had fallen. Pursuing MPs staggered. Several stopped, wrenched at their guns.

Francine's shock gave way to cold rage. She moved forward, slowly at first and then striding. Off to the left someone shouted: "Hey! Lady! Get down!" She ignored the voice.

There on the sand ahead was Zakheim's pitiful crumpled figure. A gritty redness spread around his chest.

Someone ran from between the buildings on her left, waved at her to go back. *Hiko!* But she continued her purposeful stride, compelled beyond any conscious willing to stop. She saw the red-headed figure on the sand as though she peered down a tunnel.

Part of her mind registered the fact that Hiko stumbled, slowing his running charge to intercept her. He looked like a man clawing his way through water.

Dear Hiko, she thought. *I have to get to Zak. Poor foolish Zak. That's what was wrong with him the other day at the conference. He knew about this attack and was afraid.*

Something congealed around her feet, spread upward over her ankles, quickly surged over her knees. She could see nothing unusual, but it was as though she had ploughed into a pool of molasses. Every step took terrible effort. The molasses pool moved above her hips, her waist.

So that's why Hiko and the MPs are moving so slowly, she thought. *It's a defensive weapon from the ship. Must be.*

Zakheim's sprawled figure was only three steps away from her now. She wrenched her way through the congealed air, panting with the exertion. Her muscles ached from the effort. She knelt beside Zakheim. Ignoring the blood that stained her skirt she took up one of his outstretched hands, felt for a pulse. Nothing. Now, she recognized the marks on his jacket. They were bullet holes. A machine-gun burst had caught him across the chest. He was dead. She thought of the big garrulous red-head, so full of blooming life only minutes before. *Poor foolish Zak.* She put his hand down gently, shook the tears from her eyes. A terrible rage swelled in her.

She sensed Ohashi nearby, struggling towards her, heard him gasp: "Is Zak dead?"

Tears dripped unheeded from her eyes. She nodded. "Yes, he is." And she thought: *I'm not crying for Zak. I'm crying for myself . . . for all of us . . . so foolish, so determined, so blind . . .*

"EARTH PEOPLE!" The voice roared from the spaceship, cutting across all thought, stilling all emotion into a waiting fear. "WE HAD HOPED YOU COULD LEARN TO COMMUNICATE!" roared the voice. "YOU HAVE FAILED!"

Vibrant silence.

Thoughts that had been struggling for recognition began surging to the surface of Francine's mind. She felt herself caught in the throes of a mental earthquake, her soul brought to a crisis as sharp as that of giving birth. The crashing words had broken through a last barrier in her mind. "COMMUNICATE!" At last she understood the meaning of the ultimatum.

But was it too late?

"No!" she screamed. She surged to her feet, shook a fist at the ship. "Here's one who didn't fail! I know what you meant!" She shook both fists at the ship. "See my hate!"

Against the almost tangible congealing of air she forced her way towards the now silent ship, thrust out her left hand towards the dead figures on the sand all around her. "You killed these poor fools! What did you expect from them? You did this! You forced them into a corner!"

The doors of the spaceship opened. Five green-skinned figures emerged. They stopped, stood staring at her, their shoulders slumped. Simultaneously, Francine felt the thickened air relax its hold upon her. She strode forward, tears coursing down her cheeks.

"You made them afraid!" she shouted. "What else could they do? The fearful can't think."

Sobs overcame her. She felt violence shivering in her muscles. There was a terrible desire in her—a need to get her hands on those green figures, to shake them, hurt them, "I hope you're proud of what you've done."

"QUIET!" boomed the voice from the ship.

"I will not!" she screamed. She shook her head, feeling the wildness that smothered her inhibitions. "Oh, I know you were right about communicating ... but you were wrong, too. You didn't have to resort to violence."

The voice from the ship intruded on a softer tone, all the more compelling for the change: "Please?" There was a delicate sense of pleading to the word.

Francine broke off. She felt that she had just awakened from a lifelong daze, but that this clarity of thought-cum-action was a delicate thing she could lose in the wink of an eye.

"We did what we had to do," said the voice. "You see our five representatives there?"

Francine focused on the slump-shouldered Galactics. They looked defeated, radiating sadness. The gaping door of the ship a few paces behind was like a mouth ready to swallow them.

"Those five are among the eight hundred survivors of a race that once numbered six billion," said the voice.

Francine felt Ohashi move up beside her, glanced sidelong at him, then back to the Galactics. Behind her, she heard a low mumbling murmur of many voices. The slow beginning of reaction to her emotional outburst made her sway. A sob caught in her throat.

The voice from the ship rolled on: "This once great race did not realize the importance of unmistakable communication. They entered space in that sick condition—hating, fearing, fighting. There was appalling bloodshed on their side and—ours—before we could subdue them."

A scuffing sound intruded as the five green-skinned figures shuffled forward. They were trembling, and Francine saw glistening drops of wetness below their crests. Their eyes blinked. She sensed the aura of sadness about them, and new tears welled in her eyes.

"The eight hundred survivors—to atone for the errors of their race and to earn the right of further survival—developed a new language," said the voice from the ship. "It is, perhaps, the ultimate language. They have made themselves the masters of all languages to serve as our interpreters." There was a long pause, then: "Think very carefully, Mrs Millar. Do you know why they are our interpreters?"

The held breath of silence hung over them. Francine swallowed past the thick tightness in her throat. This was the moment that could spell the end of the human race, or could open new doors for them—and she knew it.

"Because they cannot lie," she husked.

"Then you have truly learned," said the voice. "My original purpose in coming down here just now was to direct the sterilization of your planet. We thought that your military preparations were a final evidence of your failure. We see now that this was merely the abortive desperation of a minority. We have acted in haste. Our apologies."

The green-skinned Galactics shuffled forward, stopped two paces from Francine. Their ridged crests drooped, shoulders sagged.

"Slay us," croaked one. His eyes turned towards the dead men on the sand around them.

Francine took a deep, shuddering breath, wiped at her damp eyes. Again she felt the bottomless sense of futility. "Did it have to be this way?" she whispered.

The voice from the ship answered: "Better this than a sterile planet—the complete destruction of your race. Do not blame our interpreters. If a race can learn to communicate, it can be saved. Your race can be saved. First we had to make certain you held the potential. There will be pain in the new ways, no doubt. Many still will try to fight us, but you have not yet erupted fully into space where it would be more difficult to control your course."

"Why couldn't you have just picked some of us, tested a few of us?" she demanded. "Why did you put this terrible pressure on the entire world?"

"What if we had picked the wrong ones?" asked the voice. "How could we be certain with a strange race such as yours that we had a fair sampling of your highest potential? No. All of you had to have the opportunity to learn of our problem. The pressure was to be certain that your own people chose their best representatives."

Francine thought of the unimaginative rule-book followers who had led the teams. She felt hysteria close to the surface.

So close. So hellishly close!

Ohashi spoke softly beside her: "Francine?"

It was a calming voice that subdued the hysteria. She nodded. A feeling of relief struggled for recognition within her, but it had not penetrated all nerve channels. She felt her hands twitching.

Ohashi said: "They are speaking English with you. What of their language that we were supposed to solve?"

"We leaped to a wrong conclusion, Hiko," she said. "We were asked to communicate. We were supposed to remember our own language—the language we knew in childhood, and that was slowly lost to us through the elevation of reason."

"Ahhhhh," sighed Ohashi.

All anger drained from her now, and she spoke with sadness. "We raised the power of reason, the power of manipulating words, above all other faculties. The written word became our god. We forgot that before words there were actions—that there have always been things beyond words. We forgot that the spoken word preceded the written one. We forgot that the written forms of our letters came from ideographic pictures—that standing behind every letter is an image like an ancient ghost. The image stands for natural movements of the body or of other living things."

"The dances," whispered Ohashi.

"Yes, the dances," she said. "The primitive dances did not forget. And the body did not forget—not really." She lifted her hands, looked at them. "I am my own past. Every incident that ever happened to every ancestor of mine is accumulated within me." She turned, faced Ohashi.

He frowned. "Memory stops at the beginning of your . . ."

"And the body remembers beyond," she said. "It's a different kind of memory: encysted in an overlay of trained responses like the thing we call language. We have to look back to our childhood because all children are primitives. Every cell of a child knows the language of emotional movements—the clutching reflexes, the wails and contortions, the sensuous twistings, the gentle reassurances."

"And you say these people cannot lie," murmured Ohashi.

Francine felt the upsurge of happiness. It was still tainted by the death around her and the pain she knew was yet to come for her people, but the glow was there expanding. "The body," she said, and shook her head at the scowl of puzzlement on Ohashi's face. "The intellect . . ." She broke off, aware that Ohashi had not yet made the complete transition to the new way of communicating, that she was still most likely the only member of her race even aware of the vision on this high plateau of being.

Ohashi shook his head, and sunlight flashed on his glasses. "I'm trying to understand," he said.

"I know you are," she said. "Hiko, all of our Earth languages have a bias towards insanity because they split off the concept of intellect from the concept of body. That's an over-simplification, but it will do for now. You get fragmentation this way, you see? Schizophrenia. These people now—" She gestured towards the silent Galactics. "—they have reunited body and intellect in their communication. A gestalten thing that requires the total being's participation. They cannot lie because that would be to lie to themselves—and this would completely inhibit speech." She shook her head. "Speech is not the word, but it is the only word we have now."

"A paradox," said Ohashi.

She nodded. "The self that is one cannot lie to the self. When body and intellect say the same thing . . . that is truth. When words and wordlessness agree . . . that is truth. You see?"

Ohashi stood frozen before her, eyes glistening behind the thick lenses. He opened his mouth, closed it, then bowed his head. In that moment he was the complete Oriental and Francine felt that she could look through him at all of his ancestry, seeing and understanding every culture and every person that had built to the point of the pyramid here in one person: Hiko Ohashi.

"I see it," he murmured. "It was example they showed. Not words to decipher. Only example for recognition, to touch our memories and call them forth. What great teachers! What great masters of being!"

One of the Galactics stepped closer, gestured towards the area behind Francine. His movements and the intent were clear to her, interpreted through her new understanding.

The Galactic's wide lips moved. "You are being recorded," he said. "It would be an opportune moment to begin the education of your people—since all new things must have a point of birth."

She nodded, steeling herself before turning. *Even with the pain of birth,* she thought. This was the moment that would precipitate the avalanche of change. Without knowing precisely how she would set off this chain reaction, she had no doubt that she would do it. Slowly, she turned, saw the movie cameras, the television lenses, the cone microphones all directed at her. People were pressed up against an invisible wall that drew an arc around the ship's entrance and this charmed circle where she stood. *Part of the ship's defences,* she thought. *A force field to stop intruders.*

A muted murmuring came from the wall of people.

Francine stepped towards them, saw the lenses and microphones adjust. She focused on angry faces beyond the force field—and faces with fear—and faces with nothing but a terrible awe. In the foreground, well within the field, lay Zakheim's body, one hand outstretched and almost pointing at her. Silently, she dedicated this moment to him.

"Listen to me very carefully," she said. "But more important, see beyond my words to the place where words cannot penetrate." She felt her body begin to tingle with a sudden release of energy. Briefly, she raised herself on to her toes. "If you see the truth of my message, if you see through to this place that I show you, then you will enter a higher order of existence: happier, sadder. Everything will take on more depth. You will feel more of all the things there are in this universe for us to feel."

Her new-found knowledge was like a shoring up within, a bottomless well of strength.

"All the window widows of all the lonely homes of Earth am I," she said. And she bent forward. It was suddenly not

Dr Francine Millar, psychologist, there on the sand. By the power of mimesis, she projected the figure of a woman in a housedress leaning on a windowsill, staring hopelessly into an empty future.

"And all the happy innocence seeking pain."

Again, she moved: the years peeled away from her. And now, she picked up a subtle rhythm of words and movements that made experienced actors cry with envy when they saw the films.

"Nature building Nature's thunder am I," she chanted, her body swaying.

"Red roses budding

"And the trout thudding water

"And the moon pounding out stars

"On an ocean wake—

"All these am I!

"A fast hurling motion am I!

"What you think I am—that I am not!

"Dreams tell your senses all my names:

"Not harshly loud or suddenly neglectful, sarcastic, preoccupied or rebukeful—

"But murmuring.

"You abandoned a twelve-hour day for a twelve-hour night

"To meddle carefully with eternity!

"Then you realize the cutting hesitancy

"That prepares a star for wishing . . .

"When you see my proper image—

"A candle flickering am I.

"Then you will feel the lonely intercourse of the stars.

"Remember! Remember! Remember!"

OLD RAMBLING HOUSE

On his last night on Earth, Ted Graham stepped out of a glass-walled telephone booth, ducked to avoid a sweeping moth that battered itself in a frenzy against a bare globe above the booth.

Ted Graham was a long-necked man with a head of pronounced egg shape topped by prematurely balding sandy hair. Something about his lanky, intense appearance suggested his occupation: certified public accountant.

He stopped behind his wife, who was studying a newspaper classified page, frowned. "They said to wait here. They'll come get us. Said the place is hard to find at night."

Martha Graham looked up from the newspaper. She was a doll-faced woman, heavily pregnant, a kind of pink prettiness about her. The yellow glow from the light above the booth subdued the red-auburn cast of her hair.

"I just have to be in a house when the baby's born," she said. "What'd they sound like?"

"I dunno. There was a funny kind of interruption—like an argument in some foreign language."

"Did they sound foreign?"

"In a way." He motioned along the night-shrouded line of trailers towards one with two windows glowing amber. "Let's wait inside. These bugs out here are fierce."

"Did you tell them which trailer is ours?"

"Yes. They didn't sound at all anxious to look at it. That's odd—them wanting to trade their house for a trailer."

"There's nothing odd about it. They've probably just got itchy feet like we did."

He appeared not to hear her. "Funniest sounding language you ever heard when that argument started: like a squirt of noise."

Inside the trailer, Ted Graham sat down on the green couch that opened into a double bed for company.

"They could use a good tax accountant around here," he said. "When I first saw the place I got that definite feeling. The valley looks prosperous. It's a wonder nobody's opened an office here before."

His wife took a straight chair by the counter separating kitchen and living area, folded her hands across her heavy stomach.

"I'm just continental tired of wheels going around under me," she said. "I want to sit and stare at the same view for the rest of my life. I don't know how a trailer ever seemed glamorous when . . ."

"It was the inheritance gave us itchy feet," he said.

Tyres gritted on gravel outside.

Martha Graham straightened. "Could that be them?"

"Awful quick if it is." He went to the door, opened it, stared down at the man who was just raising a hand to knock.

"Are you Mr Graham?" asked the man.

"Yes." He found himself staring at the caller.

"I'm Clint Rush," said the man. "You called about the house?" He moved farther into the light. At first, he'd appeared an old man, fine wrinkle lines in his face, a tired leather look to his skin. But as he moved his head in the light, the wrinkles seemed to dissolve—and with them, the years lifted from him.

"Yes, we called," said Ted Graham. He stood aside. "Do you want to look at the trailer now?"

Martha Graham crossed to stand beside her husband. "We've kept it in awfully good shape," she said. "We've never let anything get seriously wrong with it."

She sounds too anxious, thought Ted Graham. *I wish she'd let me do the talking*.

"We can come back and look at your trailer tomorrow in daylight," said Rush. "My car's right out here if you'd like to see our house."

Ted Graham hesitated. He felt a nagging worry tug at his mind, tried to fix his attention on what bothered him. "Hadn't we better take our car?" he asked. "We could follow you?"

"No need," said Rush. "We're coming back into town tonight anyway. We can drop you off then."

"All right." Ted Graham nodded. "Be right with you as soon as I lock up."

Inside the car, Rush mumbled introductions. His wife was a dark shadow in the front seat, her hair drawn back in a severe bun. Her features suggested gypsy blood. She was called "Raimee".

Odd name, thought Ted Graham. And he noticed that she, too, gave that strange first impression of age that melted in a shift of light.

Mrs Rush turned her gypsy features towards Martha Graham. "You are going to have a baby?"

It came out as an odd, veiled statement.

Abruptly, the car rolled forward.

Martha Graham said, "It's supposed to be born in about four months. We hope it's a boy."

Mrs Rush looked at her husband. "I have changed my mind," she said.

Rush spoke without taking his attention from the road. "It is too . . ." He broke off, spoke in a tumble of strange sounds.

Ted Graham recognized the language he'd heard on the telephone.

Mrs Rush answered in the same tongue, anger showing in the intensity of her voice. Her husband replied, his voice calmer.

Presently, Mrs Rush fell silent.

Rush tipped his head towards the rear of the car. "My wife has moments when she does not want to get rid of the old house. It has been with her for many years."

Ted Graham said, "Oh." Then: "Are you Spanish?"

Rush hesitated. "No. We are Basque."

He turned the car down a well-lighted avenue that merged

into a highway. They turned on to a side road. There followed more turns—left, right, right.

Ted Graham lost track.

They hit a jolting bump that made Martha gasp.

"I hope that wasn't too rough on you," said Rush. "We're almost there."

The car swung into a lane, its lights picking out the skeleton outlines of trees: peculiar trees—tall, gaunt, leafless. They added to Ted Graham's feeling of uneasiness.

The lane dipped, ended at a low wall of a house—red brick with clerestory windows beneath overhanging eaves. The effect of the wall and a wide-beamed door they could see to the left was ultra-modern.

Ted Graham helped his wife out of the car, followed the Rushes to the door.

"I thought you said it was an old house," he said.

"It was designed by one of the first modernists," said Rush. He fumbled with an odd curved key. The wide door swung open on to a hallway equally wide, carpeted by a deep pile rug. They could glimpse floor-to-ceiling view windows at the end of the hall, city lights behind them.

"It's so . . . so . . . so big," said Martha Graham.

"You want to trade this for our trailer?" asked Ted Graham.

"It's too inconvenient for us," said Rush. "My work is over the mountains on the coast." He shrugged. "We cannot sell it around here."

Ted Graham looked at him sharply. "Isn't there any money around here?" He had a sudden vision of a tax accountant with no customers.

"Plenty of money, but no real estate customers."

They entered the living-room. Sectional divans lined the walls. Subdued lighting glowed from the corners. Two paintings hung on the opposite walls—oblongs of odd lines and twists that made Ted Graham dizzy.

Warning bells clamoured in his mind.

Martha Graham crossed to the windows, looked at the

city lights far away below. "It's so beautiful—like a fairy city."

Mrs Rush emitted a short, nervous laugh.

Ted Graham glanced around the room, thought: *If the rest of the house is like this . . . it's worth fifty or sixty thousand.* He thought of their trailer: *a good one, but not worth more than seven thousand.*

Uneasiness was like a neon sign flashing in his mind. "This seems so . . ." He shook his head.

"Would you like to see the rest of the house?" asked Rush.

Martha Graham turned from the window. "Oh, yes."

Ted Graham shrugged. *No harm in looking,* he thought.

When they returned to the living-room, Ted Graham had doubled his previous estimate on the house's value. His brain reeled with the summing of it: a sun-room with an entire ceiling covered by sun lamps, an automatic laundry where you dropped soiled clothing down a chute, took it washed and ironed from the other end . . .

"Perhaps you and your wife would like to discuss it in private," said Rush. "We will leave you for a moment."

And they were gone before Ted Graham could protest.

Martha Graham said, "Ted, I never dreamed . . ."

"Something's very wrong, honey."

"But, Ted . . ."

"This house is worth at least a hundred thousand dollars. Maybe more. And they want to trade *this* . . ." he looked around him ". . . for a seven thousand dollar trailer?"

"Ted, they're foreigners. And if they're so foolish they don't know the value of this place, then why should . . ."

"I don't like it," he said. Again he looked around the room, recalled the fantastic equipment of the house. "But maybe you're right."

He looked out at the city lights. They had a lace-like quality: tall buildings linked by lines of flickering incandescence. Something like a Roman candle shot skyward in the distance.

"Okay! If they want to trade, let's go . . ."

Abruptly, the house shuddered. The city lights blinked out. A humming sound filled the air.

Martha Graham clutched her husband's arm. "Ted! Wha . . . what was that?"

"I dunno." He turned. "Mr Rush!"

No answer. Only the humming sound.

The door at the end of the room opened. A strange man came through it. He wore a short toga-like garment of grey, metallic cloth belted at the waist by something that glittered and shimmered through every colour of the spectrum. An aura of coldness and power emanated from him . . . a sense of untouchable hauteur. He glanced around the room, spoke in the same tongue the Rushes had used.

Ted Graham said, "I don't understand you, mister."

The man put a hand to his flickering belt. Both Ted and Martha Graham felt themselves rooted to the floor, a tingling sensation vibrating along every nerve.

Again the strange language rolled from the man's tongue, but now the words were understood.

"Who are you?"

"My name's Graham. This is my wife. What's going . . ."

"How did you get here?"

"The Rushes . . . they wanted to trade us this house for our trailer. They brought us. Now, look, we . . ."

"What is your talent . . . your occupation?"

"Tax accountant. Say! Why all these . . ."

"That was to be expected," said the man. "Clever! Oh, excessively clever!" Again his hand moved to the belt. "Now, be very quiet. This may confuse you momentarily."

Coloured lights filled both the Grahams' minds. They staggered.

"You are qualified," said the man. "You will serve."

"Where are we?" demanded Martha Graham.

"The co-ordinates would not be intelligible to you," said the man. "I am of the Rojac. It is sufficient for you to know that you are under Rojac sovereignty."

Ted Graham said, "But . . ."

"You have, in a sense, been kidnapped," said the man.
"And the Raimees have fled to your planet . . . an un-
registered planet."

"I'm afraid," said Martha Graham.

"You have nothing to fear," said the man. "You are no
longer on the planet of your birth . . . nor even in the same
galaxy." He glanced at Ted Graham's wrist. "That device
on your wrist—it tells your local time?"

"Yes."

"That will help in the search. And your sun—can you
describe its atomic cycle?"

Ted Graham shrugged, groped in his mind for his science
memories from school, from the Sunday supplements. "I
can recall that our galaxy is a spiral like . . ."

"Most galaxies are spiral."

"Is this some kind of a practical joke?" asked Ted
Graham.

The man smiled, a cold, superior smile. "It is no joke.
Now, I will make you a proposition."

Ted nodded.

"The people who brought you here were tax collectors we
Rojac recruited from a subject planet. They were conditioned to make it impossible for them to leave their job
untended. Unfortunately, they were clever enough to
realize that if they brought someone else in who could do
their job, they were released from their mental bonds. Very
clever . . ."

"But . . ."

"You may have their job," said the man. "Normally, you
would be put to work in the lower echelons, but we believe in
meting out justice wherever possible. The Raimees
undoubtedly stumbled on your planet by accident, and
lured you into this position without . . ."

"How do you know I can do your job?"

"I saw it in the moment of brilliance. Well, do you
accept?"

"What about our baby?" asked Martha Graham.

"You will be allowed to keep it until it reaches the age of decision—about the time it will take the child to reach adult stature."

"Then what?" asked Martha Graham.

"The child will take its position in society . . . according to its ability."

"Will we ever see our child after that?"

"Possibly."

Ted Graham said, "What's the joker in this?"

Again, the cold, superior smile. "You will receive conditioning similar to that we gave the Raimees. And we will want to examine your memories to aid us in our search for your planet. It would be good to find a new inhabitable place."

"Why did they trap us like this?" asked Martha Graham.

"It's lonely work," said the man. "Your house is actually a type of space conveyance that travels along your collection route . . . and there is much travel to the job. And then . . . you will not have friends, nor time for much other than work. Our methods are necessarily severe at times."

"Travel?" asked Martha Graham.

"Almost constantly," said the man.

Ted Graham felt his mind whirling. And behind him, he heard his wife sobbing.

The Raimees sat in what had been the Grahams' trailer.

"For a few moments I feared he would not succumb to the bait," she said. "I knew you could never overcome the mental compulsion sufficiently to leave them there without their first agreeing."

Raimee chuckled. "Yes. And now I'm going to indulge in everything the Rojac never permitted. I'm going to write ballads and poems."

"And I'm going to paint," she said. "Oh, the delicious freedom."

"Greed won this for us," he said. "The long study of the Grahams paid off. They couldn't . . ."

"I knew they'd both agree," she said. "The looks in their eyes when they saw the house. They both had . . ." She broke off, a look of horror coming into her eyes. "One of them did not agree!"

"But they did! You heard them!"

"The baby?"

He stared at his wife. "But . . . but it is not at the age of decision."

"In perhaps eighteen of this planet's years it *will* be at the age of decision. What then?"

His shoulders sagged. He shuddered. "I will not be able to fight it off. I will have to build a transmitter, call the Rojac and confess!"

"And they will collect another inhabitable place," she said, her voice flat and toneless.

"I've spoiled it," he said. "I've spoiled it!"

MURDER WILL IN

As the body died, the Tegas/Bacit awoke. Unconsciousness had lasted its usual flickering instant for the Tegas element. He came out of it with his Bacit negative identity chanting: ". . . not William Bailey—I'm not William Bailey—I'm not William Bailey . . ."

It was a painful, monotonous refrain—schismatic, important. The Tegas had to separate its identity from this fading flesh. Behind the chant lay a sense of many voices clamouring.

Awareness began to divide, a splitting seam that separated him from the compressed contact which controlled the host. There came a sensation of tearing fabric and he rode free, still immersed in the dying neural system because he had no other place to go, but capable of the identity leap.

Bacit and Tegas now functioning together, sticking him to each instant. He searched his surroundings: twenty metres . . . twenty metres . . .

Flickering, pale emotions registered on his awareness. Another attendant. The man passed out of range. Cold-cold-cold.

Nothing else.

What a rare joke this was, he thought. What a mischievous thing for fate to do. A Tegas to be caught like this! Mischievous. Mischievous. It wasn't fair. Hadn't he always treated the captive flesh with gentle care? Hadn't he made fun-lovers out of killers? Fate's mischief was cruel, not kindly in the manner of the Tegas.

The Bacit negative identity projected terror, accusation, embarrassment. He had lived too long in the William Bailey flesh. Too long. He had lived down where men were, where things were made—in the thick of being. He'd loved the flesh too much. He should've stopped occasionally and looked around him. The great Tegas curiosity which masqueraded as diffidence to hide itself had failed to protect him.

Failed . . . failed . . .

Within the dying neural system, frantic messages began darting back and forth. His mind was a torrent, a flare of being. Thoughts flew off like sparks from a grinding wheel.

"It's decided," the Tegas transmitted, seeking to quiet his negative self. The communicative contact returned a sharp feeling of shame and loss.

The Bacit shifted from terror to fifth-order displeasure, which was almost as bad as the terror. All the lost experiences. Lost . . . lost . . . lost . . .

"I had no idea the Euthanasia Centre would be that simple and swift," the Tegas transmitted. "The incident is past changing. What can we do?"

He thought of the one vid-call he'd permitted himself to check on the centre's hours and routine. A grey-haired, polished contact-with-the-public type had appeared on the screen.

"We're fast, clean, neat, efficient, sanitary, and reverent," the man had said.

"Fast?"

"Who would want a slow death?"

The Tegas wished in this instant for nothing more than a slow death. If only he'd checked further. He'd expected this place to be seething with emotions. But it was emotionally dead—silent as a tomb. The joke-thought fell on inner silence.

The Bacit transfixed their composite self with a projection of urgent measurement—the twenty metres limit across which the Tegas could launch them into a new host.

But there'd been no way of knowing this place was an emotional vacuum until the Tegas element had entered here, probed the place. And these chambers where he now found himself were much farther from the street than twenty metres.

Momentarily, the Tegas was submerged in accusatory terror. *This death isn't like murder at all!*

Yet, he'd thought it would be *like* murder. And it was murder that'd been the saving device of the Tegas/Bacit for centuries. A murderer could be depended upon for total emotional involvement. A murderer could be lured close . . . close . . . close, much closer than twenty metres. It'd been so easy to goad the human creatures into that violent act, to set up the ideal circumstances for the identity leap. The Tegas absolutely required profound emotions in a prospective host. One couldn't focus on the neural totality without it. Bits of the creature's awareness centre tended to escape. That could be fatal—as fatal as the trap in which he now found himself.

Murder.

The swift outflow of life from the discarded host, the emotional concentration of the new host—and before he knew it, the murderer was captive of the Tegas, captive in his own body. The captive awareness cried out silently, darting inward with ever tightening frenzy until it was swallowed.

And the Tegas could get on about its business of enjoying life.

This world had changed, though, in the past hundred years of the William Bailey period. Murder had been virtually eliminated by the new predictive techniques and computers of the Data Centre. The android law-niks were everywhere, anticipating violence, preventing it. This was an elliptical development of society and the Tegas realized he should've taken it into account long ago. But life tended to be so pleasant when it held the illusion of never ending. For the Tegas, migrating across the universe with its hosts, moving as a predator in the dark of life, the illusion could be a fact.

Unless it ended here.

It didn't help matters that decisions had been forced upon him. Despite a fairly youthful appearance, the host flesh of William Bailey had been failing. The Tegas could keep its host going far beyond the normal span, but when the creature began to fail, collapse could be massive and abrupt.

I should've tried to attack someone in circumstances where I'd have been killed, he thought. But he'd seen the flaw there. The emotionless law-niks would have been on him almost instantly. Death might've escaped him. He could've been trapped in a crippled, dying host surrounded by android blankness or, even worse, surrounded by humans rendered almost emotionless by that damnable "Middle Way" and "Eight-fold Karma".

And the hounds were on his trail. He knew they were. He'd seen plenty of evidence, sensed the snoopers. He'd lived too long as William Bailey. The ones who thrived on suspicion had become suspicious. And they couldn't be allowed to examine a Tegas host too closely. He knew what'd put them on his trail: that diabolical "total profile of motives". The Tegas in William Bailey was technically a murderer thousands of times over. Not that he went on killing and killing; once in a human lifetime was quite enough. Murder could take the fun out of life.

Thoughts were useless now, he realized. He had, after all, been trapped. Thinking about it led only to Bacit accusations. And while he jumped from thought to thought, the William Bailey body moved nearer and nearer to dissolution. The body now held only the faintest contact with life, and that only because of desperate Tegas efforts. A human medic would've declared Bailey dead. Breathing had stopped. Abruptly, the heart fibrillated, ceased function.

Less than five minutes remained for the Tegas. He had to find a new host in five minutes or die with this one.

"Murder-murder-murder," the Bacit intruded. "You said euthanasia would be murder."

The Tegas felt William Bailey-shame. He cursed inwardly. The Bacit, normally such a useful function for a Tegas (driving away intellectual loneliness, providing companiönship and caution) had become a distracting liability. The intrusion of terrifying urgency stopped thought.

Why couldn't the Bacit be silent and let him think?

Momentarily, the Tegas realized he'd never before considered the premises of his own actions.

What was the Bacit?

He'd never hungered after his own kind, for he had the Bacit. But what, after all, was the Bacit? Why, for example, would it let him captivate only males? Female thinking might be a help in this emergency. Why couldn't he mix the sexes?

The Bacit used the inner shout: "Now we have time for philosophy?"

It was too much.

"Silence!" the Tegas commanded.

An immediate sense of loneliness rocked him. He defied it, probed his surroundings. Any host would do in this situation—even a lower animal, although he hadn't risked one of those in aeons. Surely there must be some emotional upset in this terrible place . . . something . . . anything . . .

He remembered a long-ago incident when he'd allowed himself to be slain by a type who'd turned out to be completely emotionless. He'd barely managed to shift in time to an eye-witness to the crime. The moment had been like this one in its sudden emergency, but who was eye-witness to this killing? Where was an alternative host?

He searched fruitlessly.

Synapses began snapping in the William Bailey neural system. The Tegas withdrew to the longest-lived centres, probed with increasing frenzy.

A seething emotional mass lifted itself on his awareness horizon. Fear, self-pity, revenge, anger: a lovely prospect, like a rescue steamer bearing down on a drowning mariner.

"I'm not William Bailey," he reminded himself and launched outwards, homing on that boiling tangle of paradox, that emotional beacon . . .

There came the usual bouncing shock as he grabbed for the new host's identity centres. He poured out through a sensorium, discovered his own movements, felt something cold against a wrist. It was not yet completely his wrist, but the eyes were sufficiently under control for him to force them towards the source of sensation.

A flat, grey metallic object swam into focus. It was pressed against *his* wrist. Simultaneously, there occurred a swarming sense of awareness within the host. It was a sighing-out—not submission, but negative exaltation. The Tegas felt an old heart begin to falter, looked at an attendant: unfamiliar face—owlish features around a sharp nose.

But no emotional intensity, no central hook of being to be grabbed and captivated.

The room was a twin to the one in which he'd been captured by this system. The ceiling's time read-out said only eight minutes had passed since that other wrist had been touched by death.

"If you'll be so kind as to go through the door behind you," the owl-faced attendant said. "I do hope you can make it. Had to drag three of you in there already this shift; I'm rather weary. Let's get moving, eh?"

Weary? Yes—the attendant radiated only emotional weariness. It was nothing a Tegas could grasp.

The new host responded to the idea of urgency, pushed up out of a chair, shambled towards an oval door. The attendant hurried him along with an arm across the old shoulders.

The Tegas moved within the host, consolidated neural capacity, swept in an unresisting awareness. It wasn't an awareness he'd have taken out of choice—defeated, submissive. There was something strange about it. The Tegas detected a foreign object pressed against the host's spine. A capsule of some kind—neural transmitter/receiver. It radiated an emotional-damper effect, commands of obedience.

The Tegas blocked it off swiftly, terrified by the implications of such an instrument.

He had the host's identity now: James Daggett; that was

the name. Age seventy-one. The body was a poor, used-up relic, weaker, more debilitated than William Bailey had been at two hundred and thirty-six. The host's bird-like awareness, giving itself up to the Tegas as it gave up to death, radiated oddly mystical thoughts, confusions, assumptions, filterings.

The Tegas was an angel "come to escort me".

Still trailing wisps of William Bailey, the Tegas avoided too close a linkage with this new host. The name and self-recognition centres were enough.

He realized with a twisted sense of defeat that the old body was being strapped on to a hard surface. The ceiling loomed over him a featureless grey. Dulled nostrils sniffed at an antiseptic breeze.

"Sleep well, paisano," the attendant said.

Not again! the Tegas thought.

His Bacit half reasserted itself: "We can jump from body to body—dying a little each time. What fun!"

The Tegas transmitted a remote obscenity from another world and another aeon, describing what the Bacit half could do with its bitterness.

Vacuity replaced the intrusion.

Defeat . . . defeat . . .

Part of this doomed mood, he realized, came out of the James Daggett personality. The Tegas took the moment to probe the host's memories, found the time when the transmitter had been attached to his spine.

Defeat-obedience-defeat . . .

It stemmed from that surgical instant.

He restored the blocks, quested outwards for a new host. Questing, he searched his Tegas memory. There must be a clue somewhere, a hint, a thought—some way of escape. He missed the Bacit contribution, parts of his memory felt cut off. The neural linkage with the dying James Daggett clung like dirty mud to his thoughts.

Ancient, dying James Daggett remained filled with mystical confusions until he was swallowed by the Tegas. It was a poor neural connection. The host was supposed to resist. That strengthened the Tegas grip. Instead, the Tegas ran into softly dying walls of other-memory. Linkages slipped. He felt his awareness range contracting.

Something swam into the questing field—anger, outrage of the kind frequently directed against stupidities. The Tegas waited, wondering if this could be another *client* of the centre.

Now, trailing the angry one came another identity. Fear dominated this one. The Tegas went into a mental crouch, focused its awareness hungrily. An object of anger, a fearful one—there was a one a Tegas could grab.

Voices came to him from the hallway outside the alcove—rasping, attacking, and (delayed) fearful.

James Daggett's old and misused ears cut off overtones, reduced volume. There wasn't time to strengthen the host's hearing circuits, but the Tegas grasped the sense of the argument.

". . . told to notify . . . immediately if . . . Bailey! William Bailey! . . . saw the . . . your desk . . ."

And the fearful one: ". . . . busy . . . you've no idea how . . . and understaffed and . . . teen an hour . . . only . . . this shift . . ."

The voices receded, but the emotional auras remained within Tegas range.

"Dead!" It was the angry one, a voice-blast accompanied by a neural overload that rolled across the Tegas like a giant wave.

At the instant of rage, the fearful one hit a momentary fear peak: abject retreat.

The Tegas pounced, quitting James Daggett in the blink-out as life went under. It was like stepping off a sinking boat into a storm-racked cockleshell. He was momentarily lost in the tracery of material spacetime which was the chosen host. Abruptly, he realized the fearful one had husbanded a reserve of supercilious hate, an ego corner fortified by resentments against authority accumulated over many years. The bouncing shock of the contact was accompanied by an escape of the host's awareness into the fortified corner.

The Tegas knew then he was in for a fight such as he'd never before experienced. The realization was accompanied by a blurred glimpse through host-eyes of a darkly suspicious face staring at him across a strapped-down body. The death-locked features of the body shook him—William Bailey! He almost lost the battle right there.

The host took control of the cheeks, contorted them. The eyes behaved independently: one looking up, the other down. He experienced direct perception, seeing with the fingertips (pale glowing), hearing with the lips (an itch of sound). Skin trembled and flushed. He staggered, heard a voice shout: "Who're you? What you doing to me?"

It was the host's voice, and the Tegas, snatching at the vocal centres, could only burr the edges of sound, not blank out intelligibility. He glimpsed the dark face across from him in an eye-swirling flash. The other had recoiled, staring.

It was one of the suspicious ones, the hated ones, the ones-who-rule. No time to worry about that now. The Tegas was fighting for survival. He summoned every trick he'd ever learned—cajolery, mystical subterfuges, a flailing of religious illusion, love, hate, word play. Men were an instrument of language and could be snared by it. He went in snake-striking dashes along the neural channels.

The name! He had to get the name!

"Carmy . . . Carmichael!"

He had half the name then, a toehold on survival. Silently, roaring inward along synaptic channels, he screamed the name—

"I'm Carmichael! I'm Carmichael!"

"No!"

"Yes! I'm Carmichael!"

"You're not! You're not!"

"I'm Carmichael!"

The host was bludgeoned into puzzlement: "Who're you?

You can't be me. I'm . . . Joe—Joe Carmichael!"

The Tegas exulted, snapping up the whole name: "I'm Joe Carmichael!" He surged along new circuits, consolidated gains. "I'm Joe Carmichael!"

The host's awareness spiralled inward, darting, frenzied. Eyes rolled. Legs trembled. Arms moved with a disjointed flapping. Teeth gnashed. Tears rolled down the cheeks.

The Tegas smashed at him now: "I'm Joe Carmichael!"

"No . . . no . . . no . . ." It was a fading inner scream, winking out . . . back . . . out . . .

Silence.

"I'm Joe Carmichael," the Tegas thought.

It was a Joe Carmichael thought faintly touched by Tegas inflections and Bacit's reproving: "That was too close."

The Tegas realized he lay flat on his back on the floor. He looked up into dark features identified by host-memories: "Chadrick Vicentelli, Commissioner of Crime Prevention."

"Mr Carmichael," Vicentelli said. "I've summoned help. Rest quietly. Don't try to move just yet."

What a harsh, unmoving face, the Tegas thought. Vicentelli's was a Noh mask face. And the voice: wary, cold, suspicious. This violent incident wasn't on any computer's predictives. . . . Or was it? No matter—a suspicious man had seen too much. Something had to be done—immediately. Feet already could be heard pounding along the corridor.

"Don't know what's wrong with me," the Tegas said, managing the Carmichael voice with memory help from the Bailey period. "Dizzy . . . whole world seemed to go red. . . ."

"You look alert enough now," Vicentelli said.

There was no *give* in that voice, no love. Violence there, suspicious hate contained in sharp edges.

"You look alert enough now."

A Tegas shudder went through the Carmichael body. He studied the probing, suspicious eyes. This was the breed Tegas avoided. Rulers possessed terrible resources for the inner battle. That was one of the reasons they ruled. Tegas had been swallowed by rulers—dissolved, lost. Mistakes had been made in the dim beginnings before Tegas learned to avoid ones such as this. Even on this world, the Tegas recalled early fights, near things that had resulted in rumours and customs, myths, racial fears. All primitives knew the code: *"Never reveal your true name!"*

And here was a ruler who had seen too much in times when that carried supreme danger. Suspicion was aroused. A sharp intelligence weighed data it should never have received.

Two red-coated android law-niks, as alike in their bland-featured intensity as obedient dogs, swept through the alcove hangings, came to a stop waiting for Vicentelli's orders. It was unnerving: even with androids, the ones-who-submitted never hesitated in looking first to a ruler for their orders.

The Tegas thought of the control capsule that had been on James Daggett's spine. A new fear trembled through him. The host's mouth was dry with a purely Carmichael emotion.

"This is Joseph Carmichael," Vicentelli said, pointing. "I want him taken to IC for a complete examination and motivational profile. I'll meet you there. Notify the appropriate cadres."

The law-niks helped the Tegas to his new feet.

IC—Investigation Central, he thought.

"Why're you taking me to IC?" he demanded. "I should go to a hospital for—"

"We've medical facilities," Vicentelli said. He made it sound ominous.

Medical facilities for what?

"But why—"

"Be quiet and obey," Vicentelli said. He glanced at William Bailey's body, back to Carmichael. It was a look full of weighted suspicions, half knowledge, educated assumptions.

The Tegas glanced at William Bailey's body, was caught

by an inward-memory touch that wrenched at his new awareness. It had been a superior host, flesh deserving of love. The nostalgia passed. He looked back at Vicentelli, formed a vacant stare of confusion. It was not a completely feigned reaction. The Carmichael takeover had occurred in the presence of the suspected William Bailey—no matter that William Bailey was a corpse; that merely fed the suspicions. Vicentelli, assuming an unknown presence in William Bailey, would think it had leaped from the corpse to Carmichael.

"We're interested in you," Vicentelli said. "Very interested. Much more interested than we were before your recent . . . ahhh, seizure." He nodded to the androids.

Seizure! the Tegas thought.

Firm, insistent hands propelled him through the alcove curtains into the hallway, down the hall, through the antiseptic white of the employees' dressing-room and out of the back door.

The day he'd left such a short time before as William Bailey appeared oddly transformed to the Carmichael eyes. There was a slight change in the height of the eyes, of course—a matter of perhaps three centimetres taller for Carmichael. He had to break his visual reactions out of perspective habits formed by more than two centuries at Bailey's height. But the change was more than that. He felt that he was seeing the day through many eyes—many more than the host's two.

The sensation of multi-ocular vision confused him, but he hadn't time to examine it before the law-niks pushed him into the one-way glass cage of an aircar. The door hissed closed, thumping on its seals, and he was alone, peering out through the blue-grey filtering of the windows. He leaned back on padded plastic.

The aircar leaped upward out of the plastrete canyon, sped across the great tableland roof of the Euthanasia Centre towards the distant man-made peaks of IC. The central complex of government was an area the Tegas always had avoided. He wished nothing more now than to continue avoiding it.

A feeling came over him that his universe had shattered. He was trapped here—not just trapped in the aircar flitting towards the plastrete citadel of IC, but trapped in the ecosystem of the planet. It was a sensation he'd never before experienced—not even on that aeons-distant day when he'd landed here in a conditioned host at the end of a trip which had taxed the limits of the host's viability. It was the way of the Tegas, though, to reach out for new planets, new hosts. It had become second nature to choose the right kind of planet, the right kind of developing life forms. The right kind always developed star travel, releasing the Tegas for a new journey, new explorations, new experiences. That way, boredom never intervened. The creatures of this planet were headed towards the stellar leap, too—given time.

But the Tegas, experiencing a new fear for him, realized he might not be around to take advantage of that stellar leap. It was a realization that left him feeling exhausted, time-scalded, injured in his responses like a mistreated instrument.

Where did I go wrong? he wondered. *Was it in the original choice of the planet?*

His Bacit half, usually so explicit in reaction to inner searchings, spread across their mutual awareness a projected sense of the fuzzy unknowns ahead.

This angered the Tegas. The future always was unknown. He began exploring his host-self, assessing what he could use in the coming showdown. It was a good host—healthy, strong, its musculature and neural system capable of excellent Tegas reinforcement and intensification. It was a host that could give good service, perhaps even longer than William Bailey. The Tegas began doing what he could in the time available, removing inhibitory blocks for quicker and smoother neural responses, setting up a heart and vascular system buffer. He took a certain pride in the work; he'd never misused a host as long as it remained viable.

The natural Tegas resilience, the thing that kept him going, kept him alive and interested—the endless curiosity—reasserted itself. Whatever was about to happen, it would be new. He seated himself firmly in the host, harnessed the Carmichael memory system to his Tegas responses, and readied himself to meet the immediate future.

A thought crept into his mind:

In the delicate immensity that was his own past there lay non-human experiences. How subtle was this "Total Profile of Personality"? Could it detect the non-human? Could it cast a template which would compare too closely with William Bailey . . . or any of the others they might have on their Data Centre lists?

He sensed the dance of the intellects within him, pounding out their patterns on the floor of his awareness. In a way, he knew he was all the captive stalks bound up like a sheaf of grain.

The city-scape passing beneath the aircar became something sensed rather than seen. Tiny frenzies of fear began to dart about in him. What tools of psychometry would his interrogators use? How discreet? How subtle? Beneath their probes, he must be nothing other than Joe Carmichael. Yet . . . he was far more. He felt the current of *now* sweeping his existence towards peril.

Danger-danger-danger. He could see it intellectually as Tegas. He responded to it as Joe Carmichael.

Sweat drenched his body.

The aircar began to descend. He stared at the backs of the androids' heads visible through the glass of the control cab. They were two emotionless blobs; no help there. The car left the daylight, rocked once in a recognition-field, slid down a tube filled with cold aluminium light into the yellow glowing of a gigantic plastrete parking enclosure—tawny walls and ceiling, a sense of cavernous distance humming with activity.

It made the Tegas think of a hive society he'd once

experienced; not one of his better memories. He shuddered.

The aircar found its parking niche, stopped. Presently, the doors hissed open. The androids flanked the opening. One gestured for him to emerge.

The Tegas swallowed in a dry Carmichael throat, climbed out, stared around at the impersonal comings and goings of androids. Neither by eye or emotional aura could he detect a human in the region around him. Intense loneliness came over him.

Still without speaking, the androids took his arms, propelled him across an open space into the half-cup of a ring lift. The field grabbed them, shot them upwards past blurred walls and flickers of openings. The lift angled abruptly, holding them softly with their faces tipped downwards at something near forty-five degrees. The androids remained locked beside him like two fish swimming in the air. The lift grip returned to vertical, shot them upwards into the centre of an amphitheatre room.

The lift hole became floor beneath his feet.

The Tegas stared up and around at a reaching space, immense blue skylight, people-people-people, tiers of them peering down at him, tiers of them all around.

He probed for emotions, met the terrifying aura of the place, an icy neural stare, a psychic *chutzpah*. The watchers—rulers all, their minds disconnected from any religion except the *self*, no nervous coughs, no impatient stirrings.

They were an iceberg of silent waiting.

He had never imagined such a place even in a nightmare. But he knew this place, recognized it immediately. If a Tegas must end, he thought, then it must be in some such place as this. All the lost experiences that might come to an end here began wailing through him.

Someone emerged from an opening on his left, strode towards him across the floor of the amphitheatre: Vicentelli.

The Tegas stared at the approaching man, noted the eyes favoured by deep shadows: dense black eyes cut into a face where lay a verseless record—hard glyphs of cheeks, stone-cut mouth. Everything was labour in that face: work-work-work. It held no notion of fun. It was a contrivance for asserting violence. both spectator and participant. It rode the flesh, cherishing no soft thing at all.

A vat of liquid as blue as glowing steel arose from the floor beside the Tegas. Android hands gripped him tightly as he jerked with surprise.

Vicentelli stopped in front of him, glanced once at the surrounding banks of faces, back to his victim.

"Perhaps you're ready to save us the trouble of an interrogation in depth," he said.

The Tegas felt his body tremble, shook his head.

Vicentelli nodded.

With impersonal swiftness, the androids stripped the clothing from the Tegas host, lifted him into the vat. The liquid felt warm and tingling. A harness was adjusted to hold his arms and keep his face just above the surface. An inverted dome came down to rest just above his head. The day became a blue stick of light and he wondered inanely what time it was. It'd been early when he'd entered the Euthanasia Centre, now, it was very late. Yet, he knew the day had hardly advanced past mid-morning.

Again, he probed the emotional aura, recoiled from it.

What if they kill me coldly? he wondered.

Where he could single out individuals, he was reminded of the play of lightning on a far horizon. The emotional beacons were thin, yet filled with potency.

A room full of rulers. The Tegas could imagine no more hideous place.

Something moved across his stick of light: Vicentelli.

"Who are you?" Vicentelli asked.

I'm Joe Carmichael, he thought. *I must be only Joe Carmichael*.

But Carmichael's emotions threatened to overwhelm him. Outrage and submissive terror flickered through the neural exchanges. The host body twitched. Its legs made faint running motions.

Vicentelli turned away, spoke to the surrounding watchers:

"The problem with Joseph Carmichael is this violent incident which you're now seeing on your recorders. Let me impress upon you that this incident was not predicted. It was outside our scope. We must assume, therefore, that it was not a product of Joseph Carmichael. During this examination, each of you will study the exposed profile. I want each of you to record your reactions and suggestions. Somewhere here there will be a clue to the unknowns we observed in William Bailey and before that in Almiro Hsing. Be alert, observant."

God of Eternity! the Tegas thought. *They've traced me from Hsing to Bailey!*

This change in human society went back farther than he'd suspected. How far back?

"You will note, please," Vicentelli said, "that Bailey was in the immediate vicinity when Hsing fell from the Peace Tower at Canton and died. Pay particular attention to the material which points to a previous association between Hsing and Bailey. There is a possibility Bailey was at that particular place on Hsing's invitation. This could be important."

The Tegas tried to withdraw his being, to encyst his emotions. The ruling humans had gone down a developmental side path he'd never expected. They had left him somewhere.

He knew why: Tegas-like, he had immersed himself in the concealing presence of the mob, retreated into daily drudgery, lived like the living. Yet, he had never loved the flesh more than in this moment when he knew he could lose it forever. He loved the flesh the way a man might love a house. This intricate structure was a house that breathed and felt.

Abruptly, he underwent a sense of union with the flesh more intimate than anything of his previous experience. He knew for certainty in this instant how a man would feel here. Time had never been an enemy of the Tegas. But Time was man's enemy. He was a man now and he prepared his flesh for maximum reactions, for high-energy discharge.

Control: that was what this society was up to—super control.

Vicentelli's face returned to the stick of light.

"For the sake of convenience," he said, "I'll continue to call you Carmichael."

The statement told him baldly that he was in a corner and Vicentelli knew it. If the Tegas had any doubts, Vicentelli now removed them.

"Don't try to kill yourself," Vicentelli said. "The mechanism in which you now find yourself can sustain your life even when you least wish that life to continue."

Abruptly, the Tegas realized his Carmichael self should be panic-stricken. There could be no Tegas watchfulness or remoteness here.

He was panic-stricken.

The host body threshed in the liquid, surged against the bonds. The liquid was heavy—oily, but not oily. It held him as an elastic suit might, dampening his movements, always returning him to the quiescent, fishlike floating.

"Now," Vicentelli said.

There was a loud click.

Light dazzled the Carmichael eyes. Colour rhythms appeared within the light. The rhythms held an epileptic beat. They jangled his mind, shook the Tegas awareness like something loosed in a violent cage.

Out of the void which his universe had become there appeared questions. He knew they were spoken questions, but he saw them: word shapes tumbling in a torrent.

"Who are you?"

"What are you?"

"We see you for what you are. Why don't you admit what you are? We know you."

The aura of the surrounding watchers drummed at him with accusing vibrations: "We know you—know you—know you—know you . . ."

The Tegas felt the words rocking him, subduing him.

No Tegas can be hypnotized, he told himself. But he could feel his being coming out in shreds. Something was separating. Carmichael! The Tegas was losing his grip on the host! But the flesh was being reduced to a mesmerized idiot. The sense of separation intensified.

Abruptly, there was an inner sensation of stirring, awakening. He felt the host ego awakening, was powerless to counter it.

Thoughts crept along the dancing, shimmering neural paths—

"Who . . . what are . . . where do . . ."

The Tegas punched frantically at the questings: "I'm Joe Carmichael . . . I'm Joe Carmichael . . . I'm Joe Carmichael . . ."

He found vocal control, mouthed the words in dumb rhythm, making this the one answer to all questions. Slowly, the host fell silent, smothered in a Tegas envelope.

The blundering, bludgeoning interrogation continued.

Shake-rattle-question.

He felt himself losing all sense of distinction between Tegas and Carmichael. The Bacit half, whipped and terrorized by the unexpected sophistication of this attack, strewed itself in tangles through the identity net.

Voices of old hosts came alive in his mind: ". . . you can't . . . mustn't . . . I'm Joe Carmichael . . . stop them . . . why can't we . . ."

"You're murdering me!" he screamed.

The ranked watchers in the amphitheatre united in an aura of pouncing glee.

"They're monsters!" Carmichael thought.

It was a pure Carmichael thought, unmodified by Tegas awareness, an unfettered human expression surging upwards from within.

"You hear me, Tegas?" Carmichael demanded. "They're monsters!"

The Tegas crouched in the flesh not knowing how to

counter this. Never before had he experienced direct communication from a host after that final entrapment. He tried to locate the source of communication, failed.

"Look at 'em staring down at us like a pack of ghouls!" Carmichael thought.

The Tegas knew he should react, but before he could bring himself to it, the interrogation assumed a new intensity: shake-rattle-question.

"Where do you come from? Where do you come from? Where do you come from?"

The question tore at him with letters tall as giant buildings—faceless eyes, thundering voices, shimmering words.

Carmichael anger surged across the Tegas.

Still, the watchers radiated their chill amusement.

"Let's die and take one of 'em!" Carmichael insisted.

"Who speaks?" the Bacit demanded. "How did you get away? Where are you?"

"God! How cold they are." That had been a Bailey thought.

"Where do you come from?" the Bacit demanded, seeking the host awareness. "You are here, but we cannot find you."

"I come from Zimbue," Carmichael projected.

"You cannot come from Zimbue," the Tegas countered. "I come from Zimbue."

"But Zimbue is nowhere," the Bacit insisted.

And all the while—shake-rattle-question—Vicentelli's interrogation continued to jam circuits.

The Tegas felt he was being bombarded from all sides and from within. How could Carmichael talk of Zimbue?

"Then whence comest thou?" Carmichael asked.

How could Carmichael know of this matter? the Tegas asked himself. Whence had all Tegas come? The answer was a rote memory at the bottom of all his experiences: At the instant time began, the Tegas intruded upon the blankness where no star—not even a primal dust fleck—had tracked the dimensions with its being. They had been where senses had not been. How could Carmichael's ego still exist and know to ask of such things?

"And why shouldn't I ask?" Carmichael insisted. "It's what Vicentelli asks."

But where had the trapped ego of the host flesh hidden? Whence took it an existence to speak now?

The Bacit half had experienced enough. "Say him down!" the Bacit commanded. "Say him down! We are Joe Carmichael! You are Joe Carmichael! I am Joe Carmichael!"

"Don't panic," Carmichael soothed. "You are Tegas/Bacit, one being. I am Joe Carmichael."

And from the outer world, Vicentelli roared: "Who are you? I command you to tell me who you are! You must obey me! Are you William Bailey?"

Silence—inward and outward.

In the silence, the Tegas probed the abused flesh, understood part of the nature behind Vicentelli's attack. The liquid in which the host lay immersed: it was an anaesthetic. The flesh was being robbed of sensation until only inner nerve tangles remained. Even more—the anaesthetized flesh had been invaded by a control device. A throbbing capsule lay against the Carmichael spine— signalling, commanding, interfering.

"The capsule has been attached," Vicentelli said. "I will take him now to the lower chamber where the interrogation can proceed along normal channels. He's completely under our control now."

In the trapped flesh, the Bacit half searched out neural connections of the control capsule, tried to block them, succeeded only partly. Anaesthetized flesh resisted Bacit probes. The Tegas, poised like a frightened spider in the host awareness, studied the softly throbbing neural currents for a solution. Should he attack, resume complete control? What could he attack? Vicentelli's interrogation had tangled identities in the host in a way that might never be unravelled.

The control capsule pulsed.

Carmichael's flesh obeyed a new command. Restraining bands slid aside. The Tegas stood up in the tank on unfeeling feet. Where his chest was exposed, sensation began to return. The inverted hemisphere was lifted from his head.

"You see," Vicentelli said, addressing the watchers above them. "He obeys perfectly."

Inwardly, Carmichael asked: "Tegas, can you reach out and see how they feel about all this? There might be a clue in their emotions."

"Do it!" the Bacit commanded.

The Tegas probed surrounding space, felt boredom, undertones of suspicion, a cat-licking sense of power. Yes, the mouse lay trapped between claws. The mouse could not escape.

Android hands helped the Tegas out of the tank, stood him on the floor, steadied him.

"Perfect control," Vicentelli said.

As the control capsule commanded, the Carmichael eyes stared straight ahead with a blank emptiness.

The Tegas sent a questing probe along the nearest channels, met Bacit, Carmichael, uncounted bits of others.

"How can you be here, Joe Carmichael?" he asked.

The host flesh responded to a capsule command, walked straight ahead across the floor of the amphitheatre.

"Why aren't you fleeing or fighting me?" the Tegas insisted.

"No need," Carmichael responded. "We're all mixed up together, as you can see."

"Why aren't you afraid?"

"I was . . . am . . . hope not to be."

"How do you know about the Tegas?"

"How not? We're each other."

The Tegas experienced a shock-blink of awareness at this, felt an uneasy Bacit-projection. Nothing in all Tegas experience recalled such an inner encounter. The host fought and lost or the Tegas ended there. And the lost host went . . . where? A fearful questing came from the Bacit, a sense of broken continuity.

That damnable interrogation!

The host flesh, responding to the capsule's commands, had walked through a doorway into a blue hallway. As sensation returned, Tegas/Carmichael/Bacit grew aware of Vicentelli following . . . and other footsteps—android law-niks.

"What do you want, Joe Carmichael?" the Tegas demanded.

"I want to share."

"Why?"

"You're . . . more than I was. You can give me . . . longer life. You're curious . . . interesting. Half the creeps we got at the E-Centre were worn down by boredom, and I was almost at that stage myself. Now . . . living is interesting once more."

"How can we live together—in here?"

"We're doing it."

"But I'm Tegas! I must rule in here!"

"So rule."

And the Tegas realized he had been restored to almost complete contact with the host's neural system. Still, the intrusive Carmichael ego remained. And the Bacit was doing nothing about this situation, appeared to have withdrawn to wherever the Bacit went. Carmichael remained—a slithering, mercuric thing: right there! No! Over here! No . . . no . . . not there, not here. Still, he remained.

"The host must submit without reservation," the Tegas commanded.

"I submit," Carmichael agreed.

"Then where are you?"

"We're all in here together. You're in command of the flesh, aren't you?"

The Tegas had to admit he was in command.

"What do you want, Joe Carmichael?" he insisted.

"I've told you."

"You haven't."

"I want to . . . watch . . . to share."

"Why should I let you do that?"

Vicentelli and his control capsule had brought the host
flesh now to a drop chute. The chute's field gripped the
Carmichael flesh, sent it whispering downwards . . . downwards . . . downwards.

"Maybe you have no choice in whether I stay and watch,"
Joe Carmichael responded.

"I took you once," the Tegas countered. "I can take you
again."

"What happens when they resume the interrogation?"
Carmichael asked.

"What do you mean?"

"He means," the Bacit intruded, "that the true Joe
Carmichael can respond with absolute verisimilitude to
their search for a profile comparison."

The drop chute disgorged him into a long icy-white
laboratory space. Through the fixated eyes came a sensation
of metal shapes, of instruments, of glitterings and flashings,
of movement.

The Tegas stood in capsule-induced paralysis. It was a
condition any Tegas could override, but he dared not. No
human could surmount this neural assault. The merest
movement of a finger now amounted to exposure.

In the shared arena of their awareness, Carmichael said:
"Okay, let me have the con for a while. Watch. Don't
intrude at all."

The Tegas hesitated.

"Do it!" the Bacit commanded.

The Tegas withdrew. He found himself in emptiness, a
nowhere of the mind, an unseen place, constrained
vacuity . . . nothing . . . never . . . an unspoken, unspeak-
ing pill of absence . . . uncontained. This was a place where
senses had not been, could not be. He feared it, but felt
protected by it—hidden.

A sense of friendship and reassurance came to him from Carmichael. The Tegas felt a hopeless sense of gratitude for the first other-creature friendship he'd ever experienced. But why should Carmichael-ego be friendly? Doubt worried at him, nipped and nibbled. Why?

No answer came, unless an unmeasured simplicity radiating from the Bacit could be interpreted as answer. The Tegas found he had an economy of reservations about his position. This astonished him. He recognized he was making something new with all the dangers inherent in newness. It wasn't logical, but he knew thought might be the least careless when it was the least logical.

Time is the enemy of the flesh, he reminded himself. *Time is not my enemy.*

Reflections of meaning, actions, and intentions began coming to him from the outer-being-place where Carmichael sat. Vicentelli had returned to the attack with induced colours, shapes, flarings and dazzles. Words leaped across a Tegas mind-sky: "Who are you? Answer! I know you're there! Answer! Who are you?"

Joe Carmichael mumbled half-stupefied protests: "Why're you torturing me? What're y' doing?"

Shake-rattle-question:"STOP HIDING FROM ME!"

Carmichael's response wiggled outwards: "Wha' y' doing?"

Silence enveloped the flesh.

The Tegas began receiving muted filterings of a debate: "I tell you, his profile matches the Carmichael identity with exactness." . . . "Saw him change." . . . ". . . perhaps chemical poisoning . . . Euthanasia Centre . . . consistent with ingestion of picrotoxin . . . coincidence . . ."

Creeping out into the necessary neural channels, the Tegas probed his surroundings for the emotional aura, found only Vicentelli and two androids. The androids were frigid, emotionless shells. Vicentelli was a blazing core of frustrated anger.

Voices rained from a communications screen in the lab

ceiling: "Have an end to it!" "Eliminate him and have done with it!" "This is a waste of time!" "You're mistaken, Vic!" "Stop wasting our time!"

They were commanding death for the Carmichael flesh, the Tegas realized. He thought of an arena, its rim dripping with thumbs: death. Those had been the days—short-lived hosts and easy transfers. But now: would he dare tackle Vicentelli? It was almost certain failure, and the Tegas knew it. The hard shell of a ruler's ego could resist any assault.

A sharp "snap!" echoed in the lab. The communications screen went blank.

What now? the Tegas wondered.

"If Bailey's death didn't eliminate it," Vicentelli muttered, "why should the death of Carmichael be any different? What can stop it? The thing survived Hsing, and lord knows how many before that."

The Tegas felt his Bacit half flexing unseen membranes.

"If I'm right," Vicentelli muttered, "the thing lives on forever in host bodies. It lives—enjoys. . . . What if life were not . . . enjoyable?"

"The death of this human has been commanded," one of the androids said. "Do you wish us to leave?"

"Leave . . . yes," Vicentelli said.

The frigid android radiations receded, were gone.

The other rulers who'd been watching through the screen were convinced Vicentelli was wrong, the Tegas realized. But they'd commanded death for Carmichael. The androids had been sent away, of course: they could have no part in a human death.

The Tegas felt Carmichael cringing, demanding: "What'll we do?"

The Bacit tested a muscle in the host's left arm, a muscle the Tegas host had never before consciously sensed. Flesh rippled, relaxed.

"Exposure means final dissolution," the Tegas warned. It was his most basic inhibition. "We must remain cryptic in colour and behaviour, impossible to separate from any background."

"We're already exposed!" It was a pure Joe Carmichael thought. "What'll we do?"

A sensation of flowing wetness radiated from the control capsule on the host's spine.

"All right," Vicentelli said. "They don't believe me. But we're alone now." He stared into the Carmichael eyes. "And I can try whatever I want. What if your life isn't enjoyable, eh?"

The sensation of wetness reached the brain.

Immediate blackness!

The Tegas recoiled upwards, fighting past the neural shock, regaining some awareness. Carmichael's neuro-system quivered and rolled, filtered out some sounds, let others through with a booming roar. The Tegas felt outraged by scraping tactility—harsh movements, rollings.

Vicentelli was doing something at a glittering console directly in front of him.

The rolling sensation went on and on and on—swaying, dipping, gliding . . . and pain.

Tegas, measuring out his attention, felt the shuttlecock entanglements of his being with that of Carmichael. Blank spots were Carmichael . . . fuzzy greyness . . . and tightly stretched threads that linked bulbs of ego-reserve. There! There! And there! Pieces of Carmichael, all quiescent.

The Bacit nudged his awareness, an inner touch like the prickling of cactus spines. Whisper-thoughts came: "Got to get out of here. Trapped. Got to get out of here. Trapped-trapped."

He was forming verbal concepts in thousands of languages simultaneously.

What was Vicentelli doing?

The Tegas felt a pulse from the control capsule. A leg twitched. He snapped a reflex block on to that neural region to resume control. One eye opened, rolled. The Tegas fought for control of the visual centres, saw a multi-faceted creation of wires and crystals directly above him, blurs of green movement. All focused on the control capsule. The host's flesh felt as though it had been encased in a tight skin.

Vicentelli swam into his range of vision.

"Now, let us see how long you can hide," Vicentelli said. "We call this the torture skin." He moved something on the control console.

Tegas felt alertness return. He moved a left foot. Pain slashed at knee and ankle.

He gasped. Pain raked his back and chest.

"Very good," Vicentelli said. "It's the movements you make, do you understand? Remain unmoving, no pain. Move—pain."

Tegas permitted his host to take a deep, quivering breath. Knives played with his chest and spine.

"To breathe, to flex a wrist, to walk—all equal pain," Vicentelli said. "The beauty of it is there's no bodily harm. But you'll pray for something simple as injury unless you give up."

"You're an animal!" the Tegas managed. Agony licked along his jaw and lips, flayed his temples.

"Give up," Vicentelli said.

"Animal," the Tegas whispered. He felt his Bacit half throwing pain blocks into the neural system, tried a shallow breath. Faint irritation rewarded the movement, but he simulated a pain reaction—closed his eyes. Fire crept along his brows. A swift block eased the pain.

"Why prolong it?" Vicentelli asked. "What are you?"

"You're insane," Tegas whispered. He waited, feeling the pain blocks click into place.

Darting lights glittered in Vicentelli's eyes. "Do you really feel the pain?" he asked. He moved a handle on the console.

The host was hurled to the floor by a flashing command from the control capsule.

Under Bacit guidance, he writhed with the proper pain reactions, allowed them to subside slowly.

"You feel it," Vicentelli said. "Good." He reached down, jerked his victim upright, steadied him.

The Bacit had almost all the pain under control, signalling proper concealment reactions. The host flesh grimaced, resisted movement, stood awkwardly.

"I have all the time I need," Vicentelli said. "You cannot outlast me. Surrender. Perhaps I may even find a use for you. I know you're there, whatever you are. You must realize this by now. You can speak candidly with me. Confess. Explain yourself. What are you? What use can I make of you?"

Moving his lips stiffly as though against great pain, Tegas said: "If I were what you suggest, what would I fear from such as you?"

"Very good!" Vicentelli crowed. "We progress. What should you fear from me? Hah! And what should I fear from you?"

"Madman," Tegas whispered.

"Ahh, now," Vicentelli said. "Hear if this is mad: My profile on you says I should fear you only if you die. Therefore, I will not kill you. You may wish to die, but I will not permit you to die. I can keep the body alive indefinitely. It will not be an enjoyable life, but it will be life. I can make you breathe. I can make your heart work. Do you wish a full demonstration?"

The inner whispers resumed and the Tegas fought against them. "We can't escape. Trapped."

The Bacit radiated hesitant uncertainty.

A Bailey thought: "It's a nightmare! That's what!"

Tegas stood in wonder: a Bailey thought!

Bacit admonitions intruded: "Be still. We must work together. Serenity . . . serenity . . . serenity . . ."

The Tegas felt himself drifting off on waves of tranquillity, was shocked by a Bacit thought-scream: "NOT YOU!"

Vicentelli moved one of his console controls.

Tegas let out a muffled scream as both his arms jerked upwards.

Another Vicentelli adjustment and Tegas bent double, whipped upright.

Bacit-prompted whimpering sounds escaped his lips.

"What are you?" Vicentelli asked in his softest voice.

Tegas sensed the frantic inner probings as the Bacit searched out the neural linkages, blocked them. Perspiration bathed the host flesh.

"Very well," Vicentelli said. "Let us go for a long hike."

The host's legs began pumping up and down in a stationary march. Tegas stared straight ahead, pop-eyed with simulation of agony.

"This will end when you answer my questions," Vicentelli said. "What are you? Hup-two-three-four. Who are you? Hup-two-three-four . . ."

The host flesh jerked with obedience to the commands.

Tegas again felt the thousands of old languages taking place within him—a babble. With an odd detachment, he realized he must be a museum of beings and remembered energies.

"Ask yourself how long you can stand this," Vicentelli said.

"I'm Joe Carmichael," he gasped.

Vicentelli stepped close, studied the evidences of agony. "Hup-two-three-four . . ."

Still, the babble persisted. He was a flow of energy, Tegas realized. Energy . . . energy . . . energy. Energy was the only *solid* in the universe. He was wisdom seated in a bed of languages. But wisdom chastised the wise and spit upon those who came to pay homage. Wisdom was for copyists and clerks.

Power, then, he thought.

But power, when exercised, fragmented.

How simple to attack Vicentelli now, Tegas thought. *We're alone. No one is watching. I could strike him down in an instant.*

The habits of all that aeons-long history inhibited action. Inevitably, he had picked up some of the desires, hopes, and fears—especially the fears—of his uncounted hosts. Their symbols sucked at him now.

A pure Bailey thought: "We can't keep this up forever."

The Tegas felt Bailey's sharings, and Carmichael's, the mysterious coupling of selves, the never-before engagement with the captive.

"One clean punch," Carmichael insisted.

"Hup-two-three-four," Vicentelli said, peering closely at his victim.

Abruptly, the Tegas felt himself looking inwards from the far end of his being. He saw all his habits of thought contained in the shapes of every action he'd ever contemplated. The thoughts took form to control flesh, a blaze of energy, a *solid*. In that flaring instant, he became pure performance. All the violent killers the Tegas had overwhelmed rose up in him, struck outwards, and he *was* the experience—overpoweringly single with it, not limited by any description . . . without symbols.

Vicentelli lay unconscious on the floor.

Tegas stared at his own right hand. The thing had taken on a life of its own. Its movement had been unique to the moment, a flashing jab with fingers extended, a crushing impact against a nerve bundle in Vicentelli's neck.

Have I killed him? he wondered.

Vicentelli stirred, groaned.

So there'd been Tegas inhibitions on the blow, an exquisite control that could overpower but not kill, the Tegas thought.

Tegas moved to Vicentelli's head, stooped to examine him. Moving, he felt the torture skin relax, glanced up at the green-glowing construction, realized the thing's field was limited.

Again, Vicentelli groaned.

Tegas pressed the nerve bundle in the man's neck. Vicentelli subsided, went limp.

Pure Tegas thoughts rose up in the Carmichael neural system. He realized he'd been living for more than a century immersed in a culture which had regressed. They had invented a new thing—almost absolute control—but it held an old pattern. The Egyptians had tried it, and many before them, and a few since. The Tegas thought of the phenomenon as the man-machine. Pain controlled it—and food . . . pleasure, ritual.

The control capsule irritated his senses. He felt the aborted action message, a faint echo, Bacit-repressed: "Hup-two-three-four . . ." With the action message went the emotional inhibitions deadly to Tegas survival.

The Tegas felt sensually subdued. He thought of a world where no concentrated emotions remained, no beacons upon which he could home his short-burst transfer of identity.

The Carmichael flesh shuddered to a Tegas response. The Bacit stirred, transmitting sensations of urgency.

Yes, there was urgency. Androids might return. Vicentelli's fellow rulers might take it upon themselves to check the activity in this room.

He reached around to his back, felt the control capsule: a flat, tapered package . . . cold, faintly pulsing. He tried to insert a finger beneath it, felt the flesh rebel. Ahhh, the linkage was mortal. The diabolic thing joined the spine. He explored the connections internally, realized the thing could be removed, given time and the proper facilities.

But he had not the time.

Vicentelli's lips made feeble writhings—a baby's mouth searching for the nipple.

Tegas concentrated on Vicentelli. A ruler. Tegas rightly avoided such as this. Vicentelli's kind knew how to resist the mindswarm. They had ego power.

Perhaps the Vicentellis had provided the key to their own destruction, though. Whatever happened, the Tegas knew he could never return into the human mass. The new man-machine provided no hiding place. In this day of new things, another new thing had to be tried.

Tegas reached for the control capsule on his back, inserted three fingers beneath it. With the Bacit blocking off the pain, he wrenched the capsule free.

All sensation left his lower limbs. He collapsed across

Vicentelli, brought the capsule around to study it. The removal had dealt a mortal blow to the Carmichael host, but there were no protests in their shared awareness, only a deep curiosity about the capsule.

Simple, deadly thing—operation obvious. Barbed needles protruded along its inner surface. He cleaned shreds of flesh from them, working fast. The host was dying rapidly, blood pumping on to the floor—and spinal fluid. He levered himself on to one elbow, rolled Vicentelli on to one side, pulled away the man's jacket and shirt. A bit of fleshly geography, a ridge of spine lay exposed.

Tegas knew this landscape from the inward examination of the capsule. He gauged the position required, slapped the capsule home.

Vicentelli screamed.

He jerked away, scrabbled across the floor, leaped upright.

"Hup-two-three-four . . ."

His legs jerked up and down in terrible rhythm. Sounds of agony escaped his lips. His eyes rolled.

The Carmichael body slumped to the floor, and Tegas waited for the host to die. Too bad about this host—a promising one—but he was committed now. No turning back.

Death came as always, a wink-out, and after the flicker of blankness, he centred on the emotional scream which was Vicentelli. The Tegas divided from dead flesh, bore away with that always-new sensation of supreme discovery—a particular thing, relevant to nothing else in the universe except himself.

He was pain.

But it was pain he had known, analysed, understood, and could isolate. The pain contained all there was of Vicentelli's identity. Encapsulated that way, it could be absorbed piecemeal, shredded off at will. And the new host's flesh was grateful. With the Tegas came surcease from pain.

Slowly, the marching subsided.

The Tegas blocked off control circuits, adjusted

Vicentelli's tunic to conceal the capsule on his back, paused to contemplate how easy this capture had been. It required a dangerous change of pattern, yes: a Tegas must dominate, risk notice—not blend with his surroundings.

With an abrupt sense of panic, William Bailey came alive in his awareness. "We made it!"

In that instant, the Tegas was hanging by the hook of his being, momentarily lost in the host he'd just captured. The intermittency of mingled egos terrified and enthralled. As he had inhabited others, now he was inhabited.

Even the new host—silent, captivated—became part of a changed universe, one that threatened in a different way: all maw. He realized he'd lost contact with the intellectual centres. His path touched only nerve ends. He had no home for his breath, couldn't find the flesh to wear it.

Bacit signals darted around him: a frantic, searching clamour. The flesh—the flesh—the flesh . . .

He'd worn the flesh too gently, he realized. He'd been lulled by its natural laws and his own. He'd put aside all reaching questions about the organism, had peered out of the flesh unconcerned, leaving all worries to the Bacit.

One axiom had soothed him: *The Bacit knows*.

But the Bacit was loosed around him and he no longer held the flesh. The flesh held him, a grip so close it threatened to choke him.

The flesh cannot choke me, he thought. *It cannot. I love the flesh*.

Love—there was a toehold, a germ of contact. The flesh remembered how he had eased its agony. Memories of other flesh intruded. Tendrils of association accumulated. He thought of all the flesh he'd loved on this world: the creatures with their big eyes, their ears flat against their heads, smooth caps of hair, beautiful mouths and cheeks. The Tegas always noticed mouths. The mouth betrayed an infinite variety of things about the flesh around it.

A Vicentelli self-image came into his awareness, swimming like a ghost in a mirror. The Tegas thought about the verseless record, the stone-cut mouth. No notion of fun—that was the thing about Vicentelli's mouth.

He'll have to learn fun now, the Tegas thought.

He felt the feet then, hard against the floor, and the Bacit was with him. But the Bacit had a voice that touched the auditory centres from within. It was the voice of William Bailey and countless others.

"Remove the signs of struggle before the androids return," the voice said.

He obeyed, looked down at the empty flesh which had been Joe Carmichael. But Joe Carmichael was with him in this flesh, Vicentelli's flesh, which still twitched faintly to the broadcast commands transmitted through the capsule on his spine.

"Have to remove the capsule as soon as possible," the Bacit voice reminded. "You know the way to do it."

The Tegas marvelled at the Vicentelli overtones suddenly noticeable in the voice. Abruptly, he glimpsed the dark side of his being through Vicentelli, and he saw an aspect of the Bacit he'd never suspected. He realized he was a net of beings who enjoyed their captivity, were strong in their captivity, would not exchange it for any other existence.

They *were* Tegas in a real sense, moving him by habits of thought, shaping actions out of uncounted mediations. The Bacit half had accumulated more than forty centuries of mediations on this one world. And there were uncounted worlds before this one.

Language and thought.

Language was the instrument of the sentient being—yet, the being was the instrument of language as Tegas was the instrument of the Bacit. He searched for significant content in this new awareness, was chided by the Bacit's sneer. To search for content was to search for limits where there were no limits. Content was logic and classification. It was a word sieve through which to judge experience. It was nothing in itself, could never satisfy.

Experience, that was the thing. Action. The infinite re-enactment of life accompanied by its endless procession of images.

There are things to be done, the Tegas thought.

The control capsule pulsed on his spine.

The capsule, yes—and many more things.

They have bugged the soul, he thought. *They've mechanized the soul and are forever damned. Well, I must join them for a while.*

He passed a hand through a call beam, summoned the androids to clear away the discarded host that had been Carmichael.

A door opened at the far end of the lab. Three androids entered, marching in line towards him. They were suddenly an amusing six-armed figure, their arms moving that way in obedient cadence.

The Vicentelli mouth formed an unfamiliar smile.

Briefly, he set the androids to the task of cleaning up the mess in the lab. Then, the Tegas began the quiet exploration of his new host, a task he found remarkably easy with his new understanding. The host co-operated. He explored Vicentelli slowly—strong, lovely, healthy flesh—explored as one might explore a strange land, swimming across coasts of awareness that loomed and receded.

A host had behaviour that must be learned. It was not well to dramatize the Tegas difference. There would be changes, of course—but slow ones; nothing dramatic in its immediacy.

While he explored, he thought of the mischief he could do in this new role. There were so many ways to disrupt the man-machine, to revive individualism, to have fun. Lovely mischief.

Intermittently, he wondered what had become of the Bailey ego and the Joe Carmichael ego. Only the Bacit remained in the host with him, and the Bacit transmitted a sensation of laughter.

MINDFIELD

In the *kabah* room another Priest failed.

It was dark in the room, which is like saying the ocean is wet. *Kabah* darkness is like no other in the universe. All radiation can be suppressed here to form a backdrop for precise inhibitory delta waves and shaped gammas.

Personality carving, it's called.

Mottled hums came from this dark, grit sounds without source-point.

The failure Priest approached death. He had been negative-thinking, permitting his accident-prayer to well up through the boundary from unconscious to conscious. In some Priests this prayer could grow too strong for Ultimate Conditioning to overcome without introducing cellular destruction into the brainpan.

But *kabah* could not kill. It could shape and twist at a sub-molecular level, but not kill. Only one solution to such an obstinate mind remained for *kabah* programming: the Priest's mind was flooded with blankness, a cool wash of nothing.

More sound trickled through the room—metallic scrapings, sharp ozone crackles without light. The failure Priest moved nearer death. Metal arms swung out where dark sensors directed, slipped the Priest into a rejuvenation tank. The tank sloshed as the body entered. The metal arms fitted caps, electrodes, suppression plates to the flesh.

Soon, a signal light would be activated, but first one more task remained. A name. It must be similar to the old name, but not near enough to rasp raw places in the dead past. And there was much dead past in this one. Many names to avoid.

Circuits flickered, settled on a single optimum sound

combination. Printer styli buzzed, graved the name on the
sealed rejuvenation tank: "Saim."

Outside the *kabah* room, the signal light glowed amber.
Another human would see it presently, and come to wheel
out the tank. Some Family would have another adult-sized
"child" to raise and train.

In all this world there were only children such as this. And
in every *kabah* room, on every priestly census scroll, all the
names were listed. Not many names remained, but they
were listed.

All names, that is, except one.

His name was George.

My name is George, he thought. *I must hang on to that.*

He felt shifting motion beneath his back, bands holding
him to a stretcher. He heard the whistling of a turbine, the
ear-thumping beat of rotors. He sensed night somewhere
beyond the pale yellow dome light above him.

We're flying, he thought.

But then he couldn't be quite sure what *flying* was . . .

There had been a long time. He sheered away from
thinking about how long a time. It was like a chasm.

And strange people.

And a tank that sloshed and gurgled around him, making
weird tickling demands upon his nerves. Yes, there'd been a
tank. That was definite.

A woman's face looked in upon him, obscuring the yellow
dome light. She turned away, and he heard her voice: "He's
awake, Ren."

A name went with the woman—*Jeni.* And a physical
appearance—moonfaced, young with blonde hair in two
long braids, blue eyes with light creases at the corners. She
wore an odd grey robe with yellow flecks in its weave. The
robe meant something. *Oh, yes—she's of the Wist Family.*

A masculine voice answered the woman: "Does he seem to
be all right?"

"Yes."

The masculine voice was Ren. He was a doctor. A dark man with almond eyes and flat features. His cerise flecked robe meant Chi Family.

"Keep an eye on him," said Ren. "See that he stays quiet."

My name is George. It was a thought like a vague handhold in darkness. *Could this be brainwashing?* he wondered.

But again he couldn't find meaning for a word. All he could think of was running water from a faucet and something foaming in a basin. *Washing.* And there were two languages in his head. One was called Haribic and came from the Educator. The other was called, in Haribic, *Ancienglis*, and this language came from . . . He sheered away. That was the chasm of Time.

Ancienglis was easiest, though.

Washing, he thought. *And faucet. And basin. And Educator.*

Educator was electrodes and ear caps and eye caps and hummings and jigglings and shakings in his mind like the rattling of dice in a cup. And passage of time.

Time.

It was like thunder in his mind.

My name is George, he thought.

"Uncle, the situation's desperate," said Saim. "There's danger more terrible than . . ." He shook his head, thinking that nothing in their world quite came up to a comparison.

"Mmmmmhmmmmmm," said ó Plar. He turned in his fan-backed oak chair, stared out of the triangular window at the water rhythm garden with its cymbaline floats tinkling in the filtered morning light. Their music was pitched to a level that could be ignored here in the Regent Priest's private office. ó Plar swung back to face his nephew. Saim straightened, standing almost at attention like any other suppliant.

ó Plar considered Saim, watching him, avoiding for a moment the crisis that now could not be avoided. He saw a few more character lines in the young face. The thin features, blond hair and light eyes dominated a weak chin. A beard would cover the chin, though, if Saim survived Ultimate Conditioning another time . . .

"Uncle, you must believe me," said Saim.

"So you say," said ó Plar. He caressed the polished surface of his staff—a long tube of metal with crooked top. His hands never strayed far from it. The staff leaned now against its slot on the edge of the desk. ó Plar tapped the metal as he spoke.

"These records you've discovered—you say they refer to many caves scattered around the world, each with its complement of . . . I believe you called them rockets."

"Weapons, Uncle. Thousands of them! We found pictures. Weapons more terrible than you can imagine."

"Mmmmmhmmmm," said ó Plar. And he thought: *The young fool! He keeps hitting the most sensitive inhibitions! Well, he's in for it now. I can't help myself.*

ó Plar took a deep breath, said: "Tell me how you found these records."

Saim dropped his gaze. Fear touched him. After all, this *was* the Regent Priest.

"Was it by digging?" asked ó Plar.

Saim shrugged, thought: *He knows we've profaned the earth.*

"Where is man's place?" demanded ó Plar.

Saim spoke with a resigned sigh: "Man's place is among the growing things on the blessed surface of Mother Earth. Neither in the sea below nor in the sky above, nor in caverns beneath. To the sea, the fishes. To the sky, the birds. To the earth's surface man. Each creature in his place."

ó Plar nodded, tapped his staff against the floor. "You recite it well, but do you believe it?"

Saim cleared his throat, but did not speak. He sensed an abrupt tension in the room, glanced at the staff in ó Plar's hand.

ó Plar said: "You cannot plead ignorance. You know why man must not dig in the earth except where the Council or a Priest-Historian such as myself has sanctified both diggers and ground."

Saim clenched his fists, unclenched them. So it had come to this.

"You know," said ó Plar. "You've seen me come from Ultimate Conditioning with the Lord's force strong upon me. You've seen Truth!"

Saim's lips thinned. *What was that old saying?* he asked himself. *Yes: In for a penny, in for a pound.*

"I know why," said Saim. "But it's not because of your holy rigmarole." He ignored the frozen look on ó Plar's face, said: "It's because back in the Lost Days people who dug in the ground accidentally set off some of these weapons. They reasoned that the region below the earth's surface was prohibited. And we're left with a law that grew out of accident and legend."

No help for him now, thought ó Plar. He said: "That would not be reasonable. And the Lord Buddha has ordered things in a reasonable way. I believe it's time to teach you this with some discipline."

Saim stiffened, said: "At least I tried to warn you."

"In the first place," said ó Plar, "there may be a few such weapons as you've described, but time is sure to have destroyed their working parts."

"Thousands of them," said Saim. "Each sealed in a giant container of inert gas. Each ready to destroy." He leaned forward. "Will you at least look at the evidence?"

ó Plar's voice grew sharper. "No need, young man. You could manufacture any evidence you needed."

Saim started to speak, but ó Plar cut him off.

"No! You came here to get me to stop the Millennial· Display. You presumed to use our relationship for . . ."

"Of course I want you to stop that display!"

"But you did not tell me why."

"I did."

"Let's look at it reasonably," said ó Plar. "Under the guidance of the Blessed Priests, mankind has grown out of its violent childhood. We've enjoyed almost a thousand years of tranquillity. Just ten days now to the Millennial Display.

Just ten days—and suddenly you've found a reason to stop that display."

"You must stop it," pleaded Saim.

"What harm can a few fireworks do to our people?" asked ó Plar.

"I don't have to tell you that," said Saim. "We've never seen such things. We're conditioned against all violence. I don't even see how you could force yourself to arrange such a display. The inhibitions . . ." He shuddered. "Loud noises, great flashes of light in the night sky. There'll be a panic!"

So perceptive, thought ó Plar. *This one was always so perceptive.* He said: "We but remind people in a relatively mild way how things were in ancient days."

"Madness and panic," said Saim.

"A little, perhaps," said ó Plar. He stilled the trembling of his left hand by gripping the staff. "The important thing is that we'll create public revulsion at the things you young rebels are preaching."

"Uncle, we . . ."

"I know what you're saying," said ó Plar. "Revive all the sciences of the Ancients! Expand to other planets! Expand! We don't even fill our present living space!"

"Uncle, that's just it." Saim felt like getting down on his knees. Instead, he leaned on the desk. "Mankind's dying out. There's no . . ." He shook his head ". . . no drive, no motive power."

"We're adjusting to the normal requirements of our Mother Earth," said ó Plar. "Nothing more. Well, we're going to show the people what it is you preach. We'll give them a display of ancient science."

"Haven't you heard anything I said?" pleaded Saim. "Your display will set off a panic. It'll be like a wave of fear following the line of darkness around the world. And the old weapons . . . they're all set to detect that wave. Fear at a critical volume sets off the weapons!"

ó Plar could feel the pressure of his own conditioning—so much more terrible and constricting than any pressures felt by the common herd. *If they only knew . . .*

"So you've stumbled on to a place of the Elders," said ó Plar. "Where is that place?"

Saim's lips remained closed. He could feel an emotion tugging at him. *Anger?* He tried to remember the angers of childhood, but couldn't. The conditioning was too strong.

ó Plar said: "We'll find the place you profaned whether you tell us its location or not."

"Get it over with," said Saim. And the sorrow he felt brought dampness to his eyes.

"I will," said ó Plar. He hesitated, sharing Saim's sorrow. But there was nothing else to do. The requirements of the moment were clear to both of them. "There is a strip copper mine in Mon'tana Province," he said. "They need an acolyte to learn the rituals from the resident."

"An acolyte? But, uncle I . . ."

"Don't think it'll lead to priesthood," said ó Plar. "You'll be digging, too. You appear to like digging."

"But . . ."

"Miners tend to be a profane lot," said ó Plar. "It comes from all that digging, no doubt."

Saim said: "Uncle, I don't care what you do to me, but won't you at least examine . . ."

"Enough!" ó Plar twisted an almost imperceptible ring on his staff. "Do you hear and obey?"

Saim stiffened to attention, feeling a terrible outrage that ó Plar should think it necessary to use the power of the staff in this. Saim's lips moved almost of their own volition: "I hear and obey."

"You will pack a minimal bag and leave at once for the Blessed of Heaven mine at Crystal, Mon'tana Province," said ó Plar. "Orders will be waiting for you at the train terminal." Again, he twisted the ring on his staff.

Saim stood rigidly at attention. The signal of the staff filled his mind with a procession of terrors without names. There was the red unthing of the black place shaping his thoughts into forms he no longer recognized. There was the slimy green part-self hearing and obeying. There was . . .

"Go!" ordered ó Plar.

The signal relaxed its hold.

ó Plar bowed his head, mumbled the litany of peace. His head was still bowed when he heard the door close. The tinkling of the water rhythm garden sounded overloud in the room.

That was close, thought ó Plar. *It's getting more difficult every day for me to deal with the accidental. My conditioning is so strong . . . so sure . . . so absolute.*

Presently, he touched a button on his desk. The semi-opaque face and shoulders of a woman appeared in a moment, projected above the desk. She wore the blue robe of a Priestess-Historian of the Brox Family. Her dark hair was tied in a severe braid across one shoulder. Green eyes stared at ó Plar from above a thin nose and stiff mouth.

"Will you give yourself up and submit to punishment?" asked ó Plar. It was a flat question, ritualistic.

"You know I cannot," she said. The answer carried the same lack of emphasis.

ó Plar held his face rigid to hide the momentary surge of loathing. *What this woman did might have an accidental necessity, but still . . .*

"Well, why have you called me?" asked the woman.

ó Plar rapped his staff against the floor. "ó Katje! You must observe the forms!"

"Sorry," she said. "I presume your nephew has just left you."

"I sent him to a mine," said ó Plar. "I gave him a jolt of the staff he'll never forget."

"You gave him just enough to make him angry," said ó Katje, "not enough to bind him. He'll run away. Your staff isn't functioning correctly today."

ó Plar started to rise from his chair.

"You couldn't catch him," said ó Katje. "There's nothing you can do. But no blame rests on you. It was an accident."

ó Plar relaxed. "Yes. An accident." He stared at the

woman, *How to phrase this?* he wondered. *I must say a thing, yet not say it.*

"You're not trying to trace my transmission signal again, are you?" asked ó Katje.

"You know we've given up on that," said ó Plar. "No. I wish to say something of the simulacrum. This accident may give you Saim and Ren and Jeni, but I will have the simulacrum. He's unconditioned!"

"I need good workers," she said.

"They're hiding near the city," said ó Plar. "Saim came in on foot. They've found one of the ancient caves, that's what. The Elders hid them with devilish cunning, but sometimes an accident . . ." He broke off. *Did she get the message?*

"How can you be sure you'll get the simulacrum?" asked ó Katje.

Damn that woman! thought ó Plar. *Directly into the jaws of the inhibition!* He said: "If you will not give yourself up and submit to punishment, there is no further need for us to talk. May you find a path of grace."

He broke the connection, watched the image fade. *Fool woman. Flying directly . . .* His thoughts dived off at a tangent. *No! Not a fool! She was testing my inhibition! When I reacted . . . that's when she knew for sure we were prepared to follow Saim: we saw the accident.*

Now, ó Plar sat back, worrying, wondering. The little signal generator he had stuck to the back of Saim's robe during the embrace of greeting—it was sure to lead the acolyte guards directly to the hidden cave. Part of him exulted at this thought, but part recoiled in horror. The careful accumulation of so many accidents . . .

George saw the door and stopped. The door had been forced and repaired. It was a perimeter door, leading to a defensive chamber. He knew that. But the ideas of perimeter and defensive chamber weren't quite clear in his mind. They came in Ancienglis, a language with big gaps in it.

Abruptly, everything around him seemed strange, as

though his surroundings had stepped out of phase with his reality. Something dragged at his ankles. He looked down at the long white robe he was wearing. It was like a . . . a hospital gown, but longer.

"Is something wrong, Jorj?"

He whirled, saw a dark man with flat features, almond eyes. *Almond eyes! Something wrong . . . dangerous . . . about almond eyes.* He said: "You're . . ."

"I am Ren, your doctor," And Ren tensed, wondering if there'd be some new violence from this simulacrum creature.

"Oh." George relaxed. "I've been sick."

"But you are well now." Ren maintained his alert, watchful attitude. *No telling what set this creature off.*

George took a deep breath.

The door!

He studied it. There were stains around it. *Blood?* He could hear voices behind it. He opened the door. It swung inward on silent hinges, revealing a chamber hewn out of grey rock. Indirect lighting gave the place a shadowless look of sterility. A man and woman stood in the chamber, talking. He knew the woman. Jeni. She came with food and sympathy in her eyes. But he didn't know the man—grey eyes, short-cropped blond hair. A feeling of youngness about him.

The man was speaking: "They didn't stand a chance of catching me. I outran them easily. And when we got into the timber . . ." He broke off, sensing the watchers.

Ren pushed past and into the room, said: "Saim, when did you get back?"

"I just this minute arrived." Saim spoke to Ren, but kept his attention on Ren's companion, who advanced into the chamber, peering around. Saim found the sight of the simulacrum freed of the regenerative tank shocking and repulsive. He said: "Is something wrong with it?"

"With Jorj? Nothing at all. He's had a hard day's problem solving and probing is all."

"My name is George," George muttered. The words were flat as though he spoke to himself.

"He speaks!" said Saim. It was a terrifying idea, as though this creature had reached a tentacle out into a new and more deeply profane dimension.

Jeni said: "He looks tired, Ren."

George focused on Saim. "You're . . ." His voice trailed off. His features grew slack. He stood silent, staring into nothing.

"Is he all right?" asked Jeni.

"Oh, yes." Ren put a hand on George's arm. "His name's something like Maid-Jor or Jorj. We found the sonal pattern by tracing a course of least lip resistance."

"Major," whispered George.

"See?" said Ren. He knew he sounded prideful, but who else had ever revived a pile of bones—created life where death had lain for a thousand years? He turned back to Saim. "You spoke of running. Is something wrong?"

"My uncle ordered me to a mine. I ran away." Saim tore his attention away from the simulacrum, wondering: *How could such a repulsive creature have so much attraction?*

"And you came directly here?" asked Ren.

"I put the grease on my shoes and around the bottom of my robe. The basenjimeters won't track me."

Fear edged Ren's nerves. "You came by a circuitous path?"

"Certainly. And I dropped through the fissure to the break under the tunnel where we . . ."

"It's different," said George. The voices annoyed him. And this place . . .

"His speech, said Saim. "It's . . ."

"Ren's had him in the Educator," said Jeni. She spoke quickly, feeling the tensions building up here, wanting to ease them.

"You should hear him in Ancienglis," said Ren. "Say something in Ancienglis for us, Jorj."

George drew himself up. "My name is Major George . . ."

His thoughts veered out into emptiness, a black, enclosing place.

"He's overtired," said Ren. "I had him in the Educator almost two hours followed by a long stimulus search session. We're opening up broad areas, but there's been no really big break-through yet." He pulled gently at George's arm. "Come along, Jorj."

George's lips moved silently, then: "George. George. George."

They went out through the door, leaving it open. Ren's voice came back to them: "That's right, Jorj, in here." Then: "Saim, I'll see you in the lab in a few minutes."

They heard a door shut.

"Where does Ren get off giving me orders?" asked Saim. He felt stirrings of . . . could it be anger?

"Saim!" said Jeni. And she thought: *Here he is starting to act jealous again.* "Ren was just in a hurry."

"Well, there's no giving of orders here," said Saim.

She touched his arm. "I missed you, Saim."

It was enough. The tensions melted from him. "I'm sorry it took so long," said Saim. "My uncle was gone when I got there. At a Council meeting up north somewhere. I sat around cooling my heels for eight days before he got back. I didn't dare try communicating. And I only had enough of that scent suppressor for one application; so I couldn't come back without abandoning our plan."

"From what you said, you might just as well have abandoned it," said Jeni. "Wasn't there anything you could do to make your uncle believe?"

"It wasn't a matter of his believing," said Saim. "Jeni, I had the funniest feeling that he believed me all right, but couldn't do anything about it. As though something within him forced . . ." Saim shook his head. "I don't know. It was odd."

"It's all politics," said Jeni. She felt . . . resentment. Yes. Resentment. One didn't feel anger, of course. But resentment was permitted. Like a safety valve. "He knows

that display will destroy all popular support for our pro-
gramme. This is just politics."

"But when I told him the display would set off a wave of
fear to ignite these weapons, he didn't react properly," said
Saim. "It was almost as though he hadn't heard me. Or
refused to hear me. Or . . . I don't know."

Jeni put down a shudder of fear, thought: *Ren should have
gone, Or I. It was a mistake sending Saim. He's different . . . not like
the Saim we knew . . . before.*

"We'd better get along to the lab," said Saim.

"There must be something we can do," said Jeni. She felt
desperate, trapped.

"You should have heard him," said Saim. His voice took
on some of ó Plar's querulous tone. "Don't you realize what
it'd mean to revive all the old sciences, you young whelp?
Don't you realize the violence and noise of just the Bessemer
process?"

"Bessemer process?"

"A way of making steel," said Saim. "I reminded him that
I was a metallurgist. That's when he first suggested I should
get closer to my work. I knew then he was determined to
send me to a mine."

"Saim! Jeni! Come along!" It was Ren calling from the
lab.

"Who's he think he's giving orders to?" asked Saim.

"Oh, stop that," said Jeni. She stood on tiptoes, kissed his
cheek. "It's just that he's anxious to get on with our work."
She took his hand. "Come along."

They went out into the hall. Jeni closed the door behind
them, barred it. They turned left down the hall, through an
open door into a square room with yellow, sound-absorbent
walls. One section of a wall was cluttered with recording
controls and playback systems. Jeni sat down in front of a
master control panel, flipped a warm-up switch.

Saim looked around. This room disturbed him for a
reason he couldn't quite name.

Ren stood almost in the centre of the room, beside a table

strewn with notes and instruments. The Doctor rocked back and forth on the balls of his feet, studying Saim's face. *Incredible,* thought Ren. *Saim—as natural as ever. How powerful the conditioning of the Priest-Historians. They take the mind and the being, and they shape all to suit their needs. And we would never have suspected had it not been for the accident and the tank we stole.*

Jeni said: "Saim, tell Ren what happened."

Saim nodded, reviewed what he had told Jeni.

"You ran away from the acolyte guards," said Ren. He nodded. "Wasn't that very close to violence?"

"I told you once I was an atavist!" said Saim.

"I've never doubted it," said Ren. "Do you think you could actually strike someone, hurt him?"

Saim paled.

"Don't be obscene!" said Jeni.

Let them learn now what it really is that we're doing, thought Ren. "I'm being practical," he said. He pulled back a sleeve of his robe, exposed a purple bruise on his forearm. "This morning, the simulacrum struck me."

"Ren!" It was a double gasp.

"Think about what is required to commit such violence," said Ren.

"Stop it!" wailed Jeni. She hid her face in her hands. *What have we done?* she asked herself. *It started with Saim . . . because I love him . . . and couldn't stand to lose him. But now . . .*

"You see how it affects us?" asked Ren. "I was never so frightened in my life." He swallowed. "I was two people. One of me was in such a panic that the little detector instrument fairly buzzed. And part of . . ."

"It detected your fear?" asked Saim.

"Exactly!"

"But couldn't that set off the weapon?"

Jeni lowered her hands from her face. "Not the fear from just one person," she said. "It takes the fear from a multitude."

"Pay attention to what I'm saying," said Ren. "I'm telling you something about this panic. It wasn't at all what you feel from a jolt of the priest's staff. Part of me was frightened, and part of me was watching. I *saw* the fright. It was most curious."

"You *saw* your fright?" asked Saim.

Jeni turned away. It hurt her to look at Saim like this. He was her Saim of old, but somehow . . . so different. So intense.

"Yes," said Ren. "At the very moment of my panic, I could consider what it meant. Violence has been all but stamped out of us. And what little's left, the inhibitory conditioning of our childhood takes care of that. But there must be something remaining because I found myself thinking that if Jorj struck me again, I'd have to grapple with him, stop him."

"Do you think you actually could have done it?" asked Saim.

"I don't know. But I thought of it."

"Why did he strike you?" asked Jeni. And she thought: *Perhaps there's a clue here to Saim's difference.*

"Now, there's another curious thing," said Ren. "Merely because I was in his path. I was questioning him about the weapons in this cave complex, trying different word-thought patterns in Ancienglis. Suddenly, he jumped up, shouted in Ancienglis: *'Out of my way!'* And he struck me aside. He ran halfway across the medical lab, stopped, turned around, and did the same thing you saw him do out there. He just . . . seemed to turn off."

"Is it possible he remembers?" whispered Jeni.

"Of course not!" Ren felt his skin tingle at the stupidity of such a question. "You know how he was constructed."

Saim said: "But, what's the difference if . . ."

"We started with a skeleton," said Ren. "Dead bones. They gave us nothing but a cellular pattern. From that pattern the *kabah* tank got the pattern of adjoining cells. A one-cell thickness. Those new cells gave the pattern for the next layer, and so on. Jorj is *like* the original, but he is not the original. The concept of memory, therefore, is not consistent."

"But those bones had been preserved by the gas from a weapon chamber," said Jeni. "There might even have been some flesh . . ." She shuddered, remembering Saim after the blast at the doorway to the cave.

"Even that wouldn't make any difference," said Ren. "This wasn't the same as growing a new arm, say, for someone injured in an accident. It wasn't even the same as . . ." He glanced at Saim, back to Jeni. "With an accident victim we have the original central nervous structure all intact. Or enough of it to give us solid patterns of the original. But with bones . . ." He shrugged.

All this talk of regeneration disturbed Saim, and he couldn't understand why. He said: "But this simulacrum was one of the Elders. Isn't it . . ."

"That's right," said Ren. "*Was.* The original died of the twenty-minute virus. There's no doubt he was a plague victim. He was one of the Elders. But the accent is on past tense of a thousand years ago. *Was.*"

Saim glanced at Jeni, back to Ren. "But he speaks the old language exactly like the tapes we . . ."

"Certainly he does!" Ren threw up his hands at the stupidity of these questions. "But we have no reconstructed memories! All we have is the pattern, the inclination, the avenues where familiar thoughts once were. It's like . . " He waved a hand in the air. "It's like a water-course. Rain falls. It strikes the earth and runs into little random rivulets. These rivulets hit the paths of earlier rainfalls, and still earlier rainfalls, until all those original raindrops are channelled in old, deep water-courses. Don't you see?"

Saim nodded. He suddenly saw more than this. *There could be dams on those water-courses. Permanent changes in the channels. Odd storage systems ready to gush out with strange twists of . . .* He began to tremble, abruptly pulled himself out of these thoughts.

"Habits," said Ren. "Old thoughts that are often repeated. They do something of the same thing. If we strike the right thought patterns, they'll slip into familiar channels for

Jorj. He'll repeat the thought or action pattern. He'll do something that was familiar because of the old pattern."

"Like striking you," said Jeni.

"Yes!" Ren beamed at her. "They were violent people. And somewhere in this violent person we've regenerated, there's a clue to the weapons in this cave system. Through those weapons we can open up all the old sciences. Think of the metals they had that we no longer have except when we melt down something of the ancients'. And the fuels!" Ren threw up his hands. He smiled at them, turned to the table, began pawing through the notes.

"It's like grasping hold of some terrible thing and not being able to let go," said Saim.

"What is?" asked Jeni.

Saim stared at her, ignoring the question, suddenly struck with the feeling that he once had known another Jeni . . . different . . .

"Why are you staring at me like that?" asked Jeni. The look on Saim's face frightened her.

"Here it is," said Ren. He straightened with a sheaf of notes. "The abstract on my sessions with Jorj. Our opening wedge is going to come from this simulacrum. I'm thinking that . . ." He broke off, focusing on his companions. "What's wrong?"

"It's almost as though I should remember something," said Saim.

"Ren, I'm frightened," said Jeni.

Ren moved to Saim's side, put a hand on his arm. "Do you feel ill, Saim?"

"Ill?" Saim thought about it. "No. I feel . . . well, different." He stared down at his right hand. "Didn't I have a scar on this hand once?"

"A scar?" Ren glanced at the hand. "Oh." Ren's voice took on a forced heartiness. "So that's it. We all have these feelings at one time or another, Saim. They pass quickly."

"Feelings about scars?"

"If not scars, some other kind of familiarity," said Ren. "It's called *deja vu*, this feeling. You'll get over it."

"When I was testing that flying machine in the big cavern, studying the manual, and adjusting all the parts, sometimes my hands seemed to know what to do when I didn't," said Saim. "Is that what you mean?"

"It may even have something to do with racial memory," said Ren. "Just put it out of your mind."

"Would you like to rest or have something to eat?" asked Jeni.

"No . . . I . . . Get on with it, Ren. Work first, rest later."

"As you say," said Ren. And he thought: *Trust Jeni to get him back on the track. I'll have to take that into consideration—the power of love and affection in maintaining a sense of normalcy.*

"Well," said Ren. He cleared his throat. "To get back to Jorj. To understand the original of this simulacrum . . ." He leafed through his notes. "Yes . . . to understand the original, we must understand the psychology of the world that bore him. There were two opposing Alliances of power in that world. They'd agreed to disarm, but for years they disarmed with one hand while arming with the other. The natural result was a sense of shame. This cavern complex is a perfect symptom of that shame. Look how they hid it. More than a hundred metres of dirt over us that has to be lifted off by explosive charges before the actual weapons tubes are exposed."

"Are we sure it was shame?" asked Saim.

"Of course it was. Concealment is the companion of shame." Ren shook his head, marvelling at the way the non-specialist could misinterpret. "And beyond this even," he said, "beyond this cave complex and the others it hints at, think of what the opposing Alliance had. Another entire network of these weapons."

"We've discussed all this before," said Saim. He was beginning to feel impatient.

"But not the psychology of it," said Ren.

"I'd rather talk about something more to the point," said

Saim. "First, what about the targets? These weapons were aimed someplace. Those targets must have changed in a thousand years."

"It wouldn't make any difference," said Jeni. "I found something horrible in dismantling some of the little guiding instruments."

"Jeni!" said Saim. "You might have exploded one of those monsters!"

"No," she said. "I didn't touch an actual weapon. I found a store of spare guidance systems. Some of them will follow lines of magnetic flux. Some can be set to go to a large area of heat or a small area of intense heat or a near bulk of metal. And you must keep in mind that all these systems are interlocking. They're made to go into a single package."

"Tell him about the other one," said Ren.

"It's a tiny version of the fear sensor," said Jeni. "When it nears a large city, it assumes command of the total guidance system. It's attracted by massive waves of fear. The fear of a populace exposed to the weapon attracts the weapon."

"There has to be some way to stop that Millennial Display," said Saim. "The wave of fear . . ." He walked away from them, turned. "People will see fireworks, all right. And that's the last thing they'll ever see."

"Maybe we should go to ó Katje and combine forces," said Jeni, "Maybe she'd help us convince . . ."

"ó Katje!" barked Saim. "I don't trust her!"

"Now, Saim," said Ren. "She's a renegade, a rebel just like ourselves. She's even transmitted pictures and data about the weapon they're studying."

"Saim, the size of that weapon!" said Jeni. "It's fifty times larger than these ones we found!"

"I don't see how she could be a rebel," said Saim. "You don't understand about the Ultimate Conditioning. I do. I've seen my uncle come out of the *kabah* room after his yearly renewal. Sometimes he looks like a man near death. We have to nurse him. You don't understand."

"Accidents do happen," said Ren. He spoke quickly,

impatient to get back to his notes and the work as he saw it.

"ó Katje's done nothing except try to force us to reveal our hiding place," said Saim. "That alone is enough to make me distrust her."

A buzzer sounded on the panel behind Jeni. She whirled and knocked down a toggle switch.

"Was that the outside warning system?" asked Saim.

"Someone's approaching the old cave entrance," said Ren. He glanced at Saim. "Are you sure you used that odour suppressor?"

"I smeared it all over," said Saim. He lifted the hem of his robe. "You can see the stains. Besides, I came in the fault fissure, not the . . ."

Another buzzer sounded overhead. Jeni slapped another switch.

"Coming directly towards the entrance," said Ren. "Saim, did you say anything to your uncle that . . ."

"Why don't you come right out and ask if I've betrayed you?" demanded Saim. He felt stirrings of unrest. *Anger?* Again, he tried to remember the emotions of childhood, and failed. The conditioning was absolute here.

"What's this?" asked Jeni. She stood up, tugged at the back of Saim's robe, removed a small disc of metal stuck there with adhesive. She extended it on her palm. "Why would you wear this decoration on the back of your robe?"

Saim shook his head, confused, feeling himself on the verge of a fearful revelation. "I . . . it isn't . . ."

"Did your uncle embrace you in greeting?" demanded Jeni. She stared at the disc on her palm.

"Of course. Family always . . ."

"That's it!" she enclosed the disc in a fist, jumped past him, ran to the door, hurled the object into the hall. Turning, she slammed and bolted the door. "Signal generator," she said. "Has to be."

"Your uncle was more clever than you thought," said Ren. And he thought: *We should never have sent Saim. Jeni or I would never have made such a mistake.*

Jeni returned to Saim, inspected his robe. "Turn around."

He obeyed, moving with shocked stiffness.

"Nothing else," she said.

A red light flashed on the panel beside them.

"They're forcing the perimeter door," said Ren.

The idea of forcing such a door seized Saim with a sudden panic. He said: "They . . ."

"It means they're using metal detectors," said Ren. "A signal generator would only give them the general area."

"How did ó Plar know Saim would try to escape?" asked Jeni. "It doesn't . . ."

"He could've planted the idea," said Ren. "We're wasting time. We'll have to run for it." He strode to the door, flung it open. *This happened because I'm surrounded by fools!* he thought.

"But what about the simulacrum?" protested Jeni. "Can he travel?"

Ren turned in the doorway. "In the flying machine. Do you still believe you can operate it, Saim?"

"Well, I've only lifted it a little bit off the floor," said Saim. "But . . . yes, I . . ."

"I'm as frightened at the thought as you are," said Ren. "But there's no other way. Come on." He turned, strode into the hall.

Saim and Jeni followed.

They could hear the hammering now, metal against metal.

They shouldn't try to force that door, thought Saim. *That's dangerous.*

"Hurry it up!" called Ren.

Everything's happening so fast, thought Saim. He felt resentment at pressures he couldn't understand.

Jeni took his hand, urged him faster.

Their way led off the big hall, down a narrow passage single file. They barred doors behind them. Dim white exciter lights blinked on at their passage, surrounding them with a pale nimbus of illumination. The air grew cooler. They came out into a laboratory cut deep in the rock. A green light glowed above a cot where the simulacrum slept. He was a green shape within green within green . . .

Saim turned away. This was the room where Ren kept the stolen regeneration tank. Something about the place loomed in Saim's mind, a black image of terror.

Why? he wondered. *Why? Why?*

"I gave him a sedative," said Ren. "We'll have to wheel the cot." He pointed to the far wall. "There's a can of inflammable fluid over there, Saim. Some of the fuel from the flying machine. Get it, please."

"What do you want with it?"

Saim's question touched a core of impatience in Ren. "The regenerative tank's in this lab. You know that!"

"But why . . ."

"We can't let them find what we've done," said Ren. "There's too much evidence around. We have to destroy it."

"What about your notes in the other lab?" asked Jeni.

"I have them in my pocket. The rest of the stuff up there won't mean anything without the evidence in here. Now, hurry it up."

Yes! thought Saim. *Destroy this place!* He said: "Where's this fluid you . . ."

A dull roar shook the room. The ceiling trembled, showering them with dust.

Ren said: "What was . . ."

"The main door," said Jeni. "We should've known. The Elders must've built one of their diabolical devices into the door just as they did in the . . ." She broke off, staring at Saim.

"What is it? What's wrong?"

They whirled. It was George, speaking in Ancienglis. He stood beside his cot, staring up at the ceiling. "Are they attacking?"

Ren answered in the same tongue, wary that this might return the simulacrum to violence. "We have to escape, Jorj. We've been discovered." Aside to Jeni and Saim, he said: "Watch him carefully. Shock awakened him from the sedative. I'm not too certain of his metabolism yet. He could do anything."

"There won't be anyone alive up there at that door," said Saim. "Whoever was . . ."

"Now it's certain we have to run," said Ren. "The explosion will attract others, and the cave's wide open."

"Where are the guards?" demanded George.

"Dead," said Ren. He darted across the lab, returned with a yellow can that sloshed in his hands.

"What're you doing?" asked George. He rubbed at his head.

"Burning my records," said Ren. "Please stand aside."

"Bad as that, eh," said George. He still spoke in Ancienglis. "The dirty, sneaking bastards!" Abruptly, he shook his fist at the ceiling. "We'll show you!"

A pungent odour filled the room as Ren poured and sloshed the contents of the can around.

"Use plenty of gas," said George. "Don't leave anything for 'em."

They retreated out of the door. Ren threw the can into the centre of the room.

Jeni clutched Saim's arm. "Saim, I'm frightened."

He patted her hand.

"Who's got a match?" asked George.

Ren took a firepill from his pocket, crushed it between his fingers, tossed it into the room. He slammed the door as a blossom of orange flame jumped up from the floor.

"To the big cavern," said Ren.

Saim turned, leading. Jeni stayed close to his side.

Ren stayed beside George. "You feel all right, Jorj?" he panted. He spoke Haribic, testing.

"Fine, fine." George answered in Ancienglis.

"He's in kind of a shock," said Ren. "We must be careful."

"Where're we going?" asked George. He felt turmoil at the edges of consciousness, but the action and need for it were central, demanding all attention. They'd been expecting the attack for a long time. Having it actually occur was almost a relief. *The dirty, sneaky bastards!* "Where're we going?" he repeated.

Ren searched in his mind for the Ancienglis word. "Helicopter," he said.

"Hope they don't have much air cover," said George. "A 'copter's a sitting duck for anything with firepower."

They emerged into an echoing chamber, large and cold. Dim exciter lights emitted a pale green glow around the room at their entrance. Still, the place remained a mass of phantom shadows.

"Well, blow the charge!" shouted George. He darted to the right along the wall, pulled down a fluorescent handle.

A crackling roar deafened them.

"Never trust a damn' shaped charge!" shouted George. "But they always seem to work." He threw another handle beside the first one.

Part of the ceiling creaked and groaned upwards, exposing a length of evening sky pale dove grey against dark green treetops. Something clanked and the ceiling stopped its movement.

Jeni pressed her face against Saim's chest, clung to his robe. "What's happening?" she whispered. "The noise . . ."

"Damn' thing's stuck!" said George. He punched a red button beside the handle. A sharp, crackling explosion shook them. The ceiling hurtled away and they heard it land in a thunderous crackle of broken trees and branches.

Jeni trembled. "What's . . ."

"It's all right," said Saim. "You knew what the old instructions said about opening this chamber. That's all it was. The explosion . . ."

"I couldn't have done it," she said.

Saim looked at Ren beside them. The Doctor's eyes were closed, his hands clenched into fists at his sides. His lips were moving in the litany of peace.

"For Chri'sakes, come on!" yelled George. He turned, ran

towards a squat black machine crouched in the centre of the chamber.

Ren was the first to follow, moved by concern for his patient. Saim took Jeni's hand, pulled her towards the helicopter.

"You've been in the flying machine before," he said. He found himself caught up by a growing sense of excitement at the thought of leaving the ground. There were remote feelings of fear, but so far away . . .

George opened the belly door, clambered into the helicopter. Ren followed, Saim pushed Jeni up on to the pipe step, clambered in behind her, slammed the door. Everything was suddenly caught up in George's urgency.

"Get a move on!" George yelled. He lifted himself up into the cockpit, slid into the left-hand seat. *Damn' civilian types*, he thought. His hands moved swiftly with an automatic sureness over the controls. "Come on! Hurry it up!"

Saim lifted up into the cockpit.

George motioned him into the right-hand seat.

Saim obeyed, watched George strapping himself in, lifted his own straps from beside the seat. There was still a smell of the preservative gas in the cockpit, disturbed by their movements.

Ren climbed up between them, stared at George. "Is *he* going to operate this machine?"

"Who'd know better how these machines work than one who actually flew in them?" asked Saim. "And I'll be right here."

"He could break down at any minute," said Ren. "You mustn't let . . ."

"Shut up!" ordered George. He pushed a white button on the panel in front of him. A grinding sound came from overhead, was replaced by a whistling roar.

Saim put a hand on Ren's shoulder, pushed him back into the cabin. "Go strap yourself down! See that Jeni's all right!"

"Here we go!" yelled George. "Look out for ground fire, and keep an eye peeled for their air cover."

The big machine jerked upwards, lurched, then rose smoothly out of the chamber. The walls slid past. Then trees. They lifted over treetops into a dove-grey sky.

Saim felt panic begin, closed his eyes tightly. *This is natural,* he told himself. *The sky is not just the place of birds.* Exultation seized him. He opened his eyes, looked out of the windows.

It was already dark on the ground, but up here in the sky it was still light. This was like living in two worlds at once.

"We're flying," he whispered.

Jeni's voice lifted from the cabin: "Saim! We're in the sky!"

He heard the terror in her voice, called back: "It's all right, Jeni. I'm here."

"I'm frightened," she whimpered.

Ren's voice came from the cabin. "Don't look out of the window, Jeni. Here, swallow this."

Saim turned, watched what George did to command the machine. Yes. Just as the manual instructed. The knob there for adjusting fuel. The big handle for tipping and turning the machine. Saim let his hands rest on the wheel, felt the movements. And suddenly the whistling of the turbine, the muted thump-thump of the rotors seemed louder.

Ren's head lifted through the cockpit door. "You must head north across the wilderness plateau, Jorj," he said. "That is the way to ó Katje's."

George lifted his hands off the wheel, looked around at the gathering darkness beneath them, at the people in the cockpit, at the robe he was wearing.

"Jorj?" said Saim. "Jorj?"

The strangeness, thought George. It was a whirling sensation in his mind. *The terrain's all different. Everything's different.*

Ren put a hand on Jorj's arm. "Jorj?"

The helicopter began to tilt left.

Saim gripped the wheel, righted them.

George said "It's all . . . I don't . . . where are we?" He rubbed his palms across his eyes.

"It's as I warned," said Ren. "Jorj had regressed. Help me unstrap him, Saim."

But Saim was too busy controlling their flight. He waved Ren's hand away from the fuel control knob. "No! Don't touch that!"

"How am I going to get him back where I can examine him?" Ren felt exasperation, knew that the drug he had taken and the medical emergency were suppressing panic. *They were in the sky!*

"Sit on the floor between us," ordered Saim. "Don't touch anything. Get Jeni to help you."

Jeni's head came through the door. "What's . . . Saim! You're running the machine!"

"You saw me do it in the cavern!"

"But that was different! You . . ."

"Here!" commanded Ren. "Stop that chatter and help me."

"Yes, of course." She was immediately all contrition.

Saim concentrated on flying the machine, Ren and Jeni dragged the simulacrum from the adjoining seat. George was slack-jawed and staring. Empty eyes. They frightened Saim as they swept out of his line of sight. He felt dampness beneath his palms.

There was full darkness in the sky now with the moon just lifting above the horizon. Saim saw village lights below to his left and far away to the right. Controlling this machine felt so . . . natural. His hands seemed to know what to do. He reached out, turned a switch. The panel glowed a dull green. Another switch. Yellow light came through the open door from the cabin.

"Thanks for the light," said Ren. He came through the door, slid into the seat George had occupied.

"What landmarks do we look for?" asked Saim.

"Where are we?" asked Ren. He spoke with a drugged dullness.

"North of Council City. I can see some village lights, but I don't know what villages. The wilderness plateau's ahead."

"ó Katje said two peaks with a lake between them," said Ren. "And a burn scar like a cross on the northern peak."

"How far?"

"She said five days on foot from Council City, but near an overtrain route."

Saim glanced at his instruments. "We could be there in only a few hours."

"Saim," said Ren, "how do you keep your sanity? I know that when this tranquillizer wears off I'm going to be hysterical." His voice lifted slightly from its dullness. "We're in the sky!"

A masculine groan sounded from the cabin behind them. Jeni called, "He's awake, Ren."

Ren shook his head, swallowed. "Does he seem all right?"

"Yes. But he's awake."

"Just keep an eye on him. See that he remains quiet."

George stirred on the stretcher, feeling the bands across his chest and legs. *My name is George,* he thought. *I must remain quiet.*

"So you're George," said ó Katje.

George leaned back in his chair, stared around the little room where he had awakened. He liked the way this woman said his name. It sounded *right,* not like the mushed-out consonants the others used. He could even hear a faint echo of the first *e*.

"Is that your name?" she asked. "George?"

She spoke Haribic. George answered in the same tongue. "That's my name." The words came out a little stiffened. Haribic was difficult at times.

The woman shifted to Ancienglis, and again he had that feeling of rightness about the way she spoke. "Is there more to your name?"

"Yes. I'm Major George . . ." The words trailed off into emptiness.

She turned to Ren standing behind her. "Is he all right?"

"Oh, yes." Ren stepped forward. He felt a great diffidence

in ó Katje's presence. It was much more than the usual conditioned reverence for Priest or Priestess. "He does this frequently, ó Katje," said Ren. "Whenever his thoughts have led him into a blank area of mind."

What are we ever going to do with him? wondered ó Katje. She studied the simulacrum. There was a roughness to his features that one seldom encountered in people.

"George," she said. "George?"

George looked at her, slowly focusing. Woman in a blue robe. Long black hair tied in a silver loop at the back. Odd crooknecked staff in her hand. Thin face dominated by green eyes.

My name is George, he thought.

I could call ó Plar and dump the whole thing into his lap, she thought. *But that would be tempting his ignorance of our hiding place. If he learns we have the simulacrum. No. The* accident *must be maintained.*

And she sensed that ó Plar could have no better solution for this Elder than she could find for herself. The creature looked so helpless in his rugged way. So attractive, really.

Ren said: "Perhaps you should question him, satisfy your mind about the fear detectors." And he thought: *How odd, this awe of her. Could she have her staff tuned to some strange new frequency?*

"What about these fear detectors?" she asked. "We found no such records or devices in this cave complex."

"But they exist, ó Katje."

"I still would like to have seen these devices and the records of them for myself. I think it odd that you should have burned everything."

"I didn't want it discovered that I'd restored . . ." He nodded towards George.

She looked at George, back to Ren, thinking: *How strange this Ren is.* "Were you so ashamed of what you'd done?"

Ren's shoulders stiffened. "I didn't think it wise to broadcast that I'd violated a *kabah* room."

"I see." She nodded, feeling a brief constriction of her

conditioning. It passed quickly and she thought: *ó Plar was right about this Ren. An odd variant on the renegade pattern. A new kind of accident.* "Perhaps there'll be similar devices and records here," she said. "We'll look for them."

"And we must act quickly," said Ren. "The danger . . ."

"So you say."

"You don't believe me?"

"I didn't say that. But you must admit you have other reasons for wishing the Millennial Display cancelled."

"You sound as though you side with the Priests on this." And he wondered: *Could Saim be right not to trust her?*

"It's one thing to follow an accident that breaks with taboo," she said. "For the sake of knowledge, of course. It's quite another thing to try to destroy the very roots of . . ."

"Accident?" He stared at her.

She fingered the slim central ring on her staff, and Ren felt the ripple of nervous disquiet that always preceded a heavy taste of displeasure.

"Please," he petitioned her.

"I would hate to return you to a full course of conditioning," she said. And she thought: *We'll have to do it, of course. As soon as we've exhausted our need for his accidental talents.*

Ren paled. "ó Katje, I . . ."

"It doesn't please me to have to emphasize my words with the staff," she said.

"Of course, ó Katje." He found that he was trembling. There were dim recollections in his mind of a full course of reconditioning. Darkness. Fearful twistings of semi-consciousness. Terrors!

ó Katje looked down at George. "Now, Ren, tell me your purpose with this simulacrum."

"Yes, ó Katje." He stilled the trembling. "It seemed logical. The bones were intact and in a wonderful state of preservation because of the gas."

"Gas?"

"From a weapon chamber."

"Ah, the inert substance, the preservative."

"Yes. There'd been some sort of accident to the chamber. And there was only one set of bones. I knew from medical use of the simpler tanks that the *kabah* tank could reproduce a cellular pattern in its full stage of . . ."

"This is all very interesting, dear Ren, but it's confined to *methods* when I'm more interested in your purpose."

"Yes, of course." He found that his right eyelid was twitching, rubbed it. "Purpose. I felt that we could restore many of the old habit channels in such a being—the compulsives, certainly, and the overriding repetitives—and from them gain clues to the working of the ancient devices."

She spoke through a haze of inhibitory shock: "And you restored such channels?"

Ren missed the stiffness of her voice, said: "There are signs. I think we're on the verge of a breakthrough. If we once restored his full name, perhaps . . ."

"How could you?" She almost screeched the words.

He stared at her. "ó Katje, what's . . ."

"The pains of such recall," she said. "The recollection of his actual moment of death!"

"But ó Katje, it's not exactly memories we . . ."

"A quibble! Have you no inhibitions at all?"

"ó Katje, I don't . . ."

"That which the Lord has taken unto Himself completes the Circle of Karma," she said. "You've not only invaded this domain, you . . ."

"But you *knew* this, ó Katje!"

"There's a difference in knowing an abstract idea and seeing the very substance of it," she said.

"Simulacrum," said George.

They turned, looked at him.

"Simulacrum?" asked George. All this talk-talk between the beautiful dark woman and the doctor. It had dawned on George that simulacrum referred to himself. And in his Educator-memory was a definition: *Sham. Something vague and unreal.*

"I'm no simulacrum," he said. "I'm real."

ó Katje drew in a trembling breath. "And that, Ren, is the thing which overshadows all else. He is real. He is real. He is real. And you would have him recall all his past, all his name, all . . ."

"My name?" said George. "It's Major George . . ." His thoughts shot out into the emptiness. There was no mindhold here, no place of orientation. But he knew he had been here before. There were faces, words, names, sensations.

Somewhere distant and subdued he heard a woman's voice. "You see, Ren? Have you any idea how constricting the inhibitions of a Priestess can be? Have you even the faintest conception?"

But that was away somewhere. This place in his mind, this was *here*. And there were old, familiar-feeling things. So many faces. And insistent voices: "And don't forget to bring home a dozen eggs. We're having omelet . . . Daddy, can I have a new dress for my birthday? . . . If you're the last man in the missile post and condition red is signalled, what is the procedure? . . . But I've got to know what's happened to my family! I've got to know!"

Within his mind, George stared at that last speaker, recognizing the face. *It was himself!* He was like a puppet standing in front of a visiphone, shouting into it at the uniformed man on the other end. *Man? Sure—Colonel Larkin!* "Pullyourselftogetherman!" the Colonel was yelling. "You're a soldier, you hear? You have your duty to do! Now, do it! Fire Betsy and Mabel! At once, you hear?" The Colonel paled, clutched at his throat. "May Day, you fool! People are dying like flies out here. The Ruskies have sneaked in a . . ." The Colonel supported himself on the phone stand. "Major Kinder, I order you to do your duty. Fire Betsy and . . ." He slumped out of sight.

George pushed himself out of the chair. He saw a tall woman, a figure in another world. She stepped aside.

Fire Betsy and Mabel.

The room seemed unfamiliar. Oh, sure. There was the

door. These missile post doors were all the same. He'd forgotten for a moment that they'd escaped to another post. In a 'copter. The first post had been under attack. That's what the Colonel was talking about, of course. *May Day. Fire Betsy and Mabel.*

George crossed to the door, opened it.

"What's he doing?" It was the female voice behind him. The sound barely registered.

"He's living out some ancient habit pattern." It was a man's voice. Ren. But Ren was part of an unreal world. This was now. This was urgent.

George heard footsteps padding behind as he emerged into a hall, turned left towards an open door where he could see part of an instrument panel with a sigalert screen. *Fire Betsy and Mabel.* There was an image in his mind—giant grey tubes with sleek delta fins. The big ones. The city-wreckers.

He entered the room with the instrument panel, still dimly conscious of the footsteps following. And distant voices: "What's he doing in here? Shouldn't we stop him? Would it hurt him if we interfered?"

Better not interfere, thought George. He glanced around. There was a difference in the room, a difference in the controls on the panels. But it was difference that he recognized. This was a command post. One of the big centrals. The sequence panel held remote control segments for radio and radar direction of any bird in the entire defence complex. There were overrides. Salvo controls. Barrage. The master console was the newer type with contour handles instead of the old knobbed ones. The anchored chair in Command-Central position held a power arm.

Two people stepped aside as he crossed to the chair, slid into it. Names flitted through his mind: *Jeni. Saim.* He coded the board for recognition to bypass the booby-traps, tested for power. A light glowed in front of him.

"He's turned on a power source." That was Jeni.

"But nothing happened! Nothing exploded!" That was ó Katje.

"He did something first," said Jeni.

"Do these things still have power?" That was Ren.

"Dry capacitors, sun-charged," said Jeni. "Virtually ageless in their preservative."

"Be quiet!" snapped George. He activated the dry-run circuit tester. The board went green except for two plates in the lower left. One indicated firing chamber evacuated of gas. The other showed activity in the firing chamber. George rapped the plates. They remained dead. There couldn't be anything wrong with the birds, he knew. The rest of the board was green.

"I think we'd better stop him," said ó Katje. She felt a moiling war of inhibitions within. Nerves cried for action, were stopped. To interfere with this real-simulacrum might injure him-it. But there was a deadly directness in George's actions that told her what he was doing. He was getting ready to explode those terrible weapon tubes!

"Is he getting ready to set off one of those weapons?" asked Jeni.

"They used collapsed atom energy," said Ren. "It doesn't seem likely he'd . . ."

"I told you to be quiet!" said George. He indicated the dead plates on the board. "Can't those fools get out of there!" He punched the twenty-second warning, felt the dull clamour of it through his feet.

"What's that?" asked Saim.

"Can't those fools hear the warning?" asked George. "Do they want to be burned to cinders?"

ó Katje tottered forward, fighting her inhibitions. She put a hand on George's arm, pulling it as he started to move it towards a red handle on the panel. "Please, George, you must not do . . ."

He struck without warning. One instant he was sitting in the chair, intent on the panel. The next instant he was out of the chair, punching.

ó Katje fell beside the chair. Ren was knocked against a side wall, sagged to the floor. Jeni moved to interfere, and a fist to the side of her head sent her reeling.

Through blurred vision, Jeni saw Saim retrieve ó Katje's staff from the floor, raise it. Jeni staggered sideways, only half conscious, but still able to see Saim bring the staff crashing down on George's head. The look in his eyes as he delivered the blow was almost as terrifying to Jeni as was awareness of the violence itself.

Jeni slumped to the floor, pressing her hands to her eyes.

A shuddery silence settled over the room, then Saim was at her side, cradling her head: "Jeni! My dear, did he hurt you?"

His touch was both repellent and seductive. She started to push him away, felt her palm against his neck. The next instant, they were kissing with a passion that blocked out virtually all other sensation.

So violent! she thought. *So wonderfully violent!*

Saim pulled back, caressed her cheek.

"Saim," she whispered. Then, as memory of violence flooded back into her mind. "You hit him!"

"I saw him hurt you," said Saim. "I don't know. I couldn't let him hurt you."

ó Plar stared down the length of the narrow work table at ó Katje. Yellow light from a ceiling fixture bathed the centre of the table, reflected up into the faces of Ren, Jeni and Saim. ó Katje held a cold compress against her jaw. Purple bruises marked Ren's jaw and Jeni's cheek. Only Saim appeared unmarked, except for a cold, staring look about the eyes.

A feeling of sadness and futility filled ó Plar. How long would it be until another accidental set of circumstances combined in a chain such as this one? A Priestess who could dig and explore antiquities without inhibition—would there ever again be another such as ó Katje? And Ren, who had stolen a *kabah* tank, and revived a virtually uninhibited ancient—how could they ever hope to happen on such a sequence ever again?

ó Plar sighed, spoke with deceptive mildness: "ó Katje, you knew it would tempt my ignorance of your hideaway to bring the simulacrum here. Could you not have been satisfied with Ren and Jeni and Saim?"

"I didn't bring the creature here." The movement of her mouth sent pains from her jaw up the side of her head. She grimaced.

"The path of the air machine was marked," said ó Plar. "We couldn't fail to note the direction and then it was simply a matter of localization. You must've known this."

"I tell you I didn't bring them here," said ó Katje. Again, she winced at the pain. She shared some of ó Plar's feeling of futility, but it was tempered by something she could only call negative-emotion. It couldn't be resentment, certainly. But if ó Plar had only waited! The situation had been filled with such accident potential!

"So it was all some kind of trickery," said Saim.

ó Plar tapped his staff against the table for emphasis, said: "You will not discuss what you fail to understand." He kept his attention on ó Katje. "Look at what has happened, ó Katje. The violence. The defilement. Is it any wonder that I . . ."

"You could have waited," she said. And she realized that it *was* resentment she felt. The violence was to blame, of course. It upset every inhibitory balance.

Saim slammed his palm against the table-top, watched the shocked reactions. He could feel something building up within himself. It had something to do with the violence and the dark memories.

"You haven't said anything about my striking the simulacrum," he said.

Again ó Plar tapped his staff against the table. "Saim, must I silence you?"

I could grab the staff away from him, break it before he realized what was happening, thought Saim. And he sank back in his seat, shocked to stillness by the thought. *What is happening to me?* he wondered.

"So," said ó Plar. "Ren, bring your simulacrum from the other room, please."

Ren stood up obediently, left the room. All he could think was: *The shame! The shame! Oh, the shame!*

Jeni reached across the space between their chairs, took Saim's hand. *I started this,* she thought. She looked sidelong at Saim. *Because I refused to lose him. That's when it started. If Ren hadn't already smuggled a rejuvenation tank into the cave, he'd never have thought about building life into Jorj's bones.*

"In a way, we should be glad it's over," said ó Plar. "I'm beginning to see that violence serves no reasonable purpose."

"That's your inhibitions speaking," said ó Katje. "Anyway violence doesn't have to be reasonable." And she thought: *There's a thing we've learned today—the attraction of being unreasonable.*

Ren came back leading George.

"Seat him here by me," said ó Plar. He gestured to an empty chair at his right.

I am called George, George thought. *Major George Kinder, USAF. USAF? That meant something important, but he couldn't fix it to any association. Uniform? More nonsense.* He realized someone was leading him into a room with people. The back of his head throbbed. Pain. And the yellow light hurt his eyes. He sank gratefully into a chair.

"You all have forced a most painful lesson upon yourselves," said ó Plar. "I wish no one to leave this room. You will watch while I do a terrible thing that must be done."

Ren stood behind George's chair. "What are you going to do?" He felt suddenly fearful, cowed by a sense of enormous guilt.

"I am going to awaken the ancient memories," said ó Plar.

Ren stared wildly around the table. "Memories? You mustn't!"

"Part of a man cannot be reconditioned," said ó Plar. "Would you have me destroy him?"

ó Plar felt the weariness in his bones, sighed. So much that could have happened here, and now no alternative but to level it all down to the great common inhibition. No help for it at all. The strictures of his own conditioning were too severe to hope for any other solution.

"But it's just a simulacrum," protested Ren. The terror welling in his mind threatened to overwhelm him.

"You will sit down here on my left where you may watch your simulacrum's face," said ó Plar. He gestured with the staff, kept it aimed at Ren while the doctor obeyed. "Now," said ó Plar, "this is a human being. We will start with that. Ren doesn't want to talk about memories because if he did he'd have to consider this creature more than simulacrum."

"Please?" said Ren.

"I will not warn you again," said ó Plar.

George leaned forward, ignoring the pain in his head. He could feel deep anger against these people, dark and obscure currents surging within himself. "What are you talking about?" he demanded.

ó Plar said: "George, who are we, we people seated around this table?"

George felt rage mingled with frustration. A word came into his mind. "You're Russians!"

ó Plar shook his head. "There are no Russians any more. Or members of any other citizen state." He gestured at his robe, his staff. "Look at me."

George looked—the robe. He glanced around the table, back to ó Plar. Fear kept him silent. The strangeness . . .

"Do we look like anyone you've ever seen?"

George shook his head. *I'm having a nightmare,* he thought. "No," he said.

ó Plar said: "It's been a thousand years since you died, George."

George sat silently staring, unable to face the word or escape it.

A shocked gasp echoed around the table.

"ó Plar?" whispered ó Katje.

"Face it together, all of you," said ó Plar.

"Died?" whispered George.

"You died," said ó Plar. "The pattern is within your mind. The circle complete. I will recall it for you from the account of Pollima, the great historian."

"ó Plar," said Saim. "Uncle, don't you think you should . . ."

"There's no more accurate account," said ó Plar. "A wonderfully terrible account from an eye-witness. Child at the time, of course."

Saim felt the stirrings of vague memories. "But, Uncle . . ."

"What do you mean DIED?" roared George.

"Listen," said ó Plar. "You felt dizzy, then extremely hot. Your vision blurred. You found it difficult to breathe. You most likely clutched at your throat. You heard your own heart beating. It was like a giant drum in your head. Then you fell unconscious. Then you died. The whole process took about twenty minutes. That's why we refer to it historically as the twenty-minute virus."

I was in the hallway from communications to the control chamber, George thought. *I saw Vince's body sprawled halfway out of the door to the ready room. His face was mottled black with the veins all dark. It was the most terrifying thing I'd ever seen. But the Colonel had just told me to fire Betsy and Mabel. I stepped around Vince's body and headed for the panel. That's when I suddenly felt dizzy.*

"I felt dizzy," he said.

"That's correct," said ó Plar. And he glanced at the frozen shocked faces around the table. *Let them see what they have revived,* he thought. He turned back to the figure of George. "If there was anyone near to hear you, you probably said you were dizzy. Pollima's father was a doctor. That's what he said. He described his symptoms to her as he died. A truly heroic action."

"Hot," said George. "Sweat's pouring off me."

"And what do you see?" asked ó Plar.

"Everything's going blurred," he said. "Like it was under water." The tendons stood out on his neck. His chest strained upwards, collapsed . . . strained upwards, collapsed. "Can't . . . breathe. My chest. Pain. My God! What's that pounding . . . that pounding . . ."

A hand came past ó Plar as Ren slapped a hypoject on to George's neck.

"Thank you, Ren," said ó Plar. "I was about to request that." He stared at George's face, the jaw sagging in unconsciousness. "I imagine that's burned all the old memory channels back into place. One's life pattern tends to be linked to this trauma."

How right he is, thought Saim.

"You . . . monster," whispered Ren.

ó Plar glanced at the doctor. "Me? You malign me. I did a necessary thing, and I'll pay for it much more heavily than you'll pay for what you did. *You* don't have to re-experience Ultimate Conditioning once a year."

ó Katje dropped the compress from her jaw. "ó Plar! I did not think . . . ohhhh . . ."

"Yes, a terrible thing to take into the *kabah* room," said ó Plar. "I most likely won't survive it."

Saim got to his feet. All during ó Plar's recital he had felt darkness peeling away from his mind like onion skins. He felt terrified and exalted. *Kabah* room without end down a corridor of time. Each constricting the will, subjecting the individual life to a dull pattern of placidity.

"I died," whispered George.

"Only once," said Saim. "I've died times without number." He glanced at ó Plar. "In the *kabah* room eh, *Uncle?*"

"Saim!" ó Plar raised his staff.

In one stride, Saim was beside ó Plar, wrenched the staff from still old fingers and smashed it against the table.

"There was no Millennial Display planned, was there, *Uncle?*" demanded Saim.

ó Plar drew himself up in frozen dignity. "We had every reason to suspect an accident would . . ."

"One rocket is all it'd take, eh, Uncle?" Saim glanced at the others in the room, patted Jeni's shoulder. "One rocket.

Other rockets are keyed to defensive systems and would go up to knock down an invading rocket. Fear would take care of the rest."

Jeni said: "Saim, you're frightening me!"

"The whole world's like a mindfield, eh, *Uncle?*" asked Saim. "Just waiting to be set off."

George straightened, spoke more strongly. "I died. You said . . . virus." He glanced up at Saim, then at the others. "You must be descended from whoever started it."

ó Plar said: "Saim, I don't understand. The Ultimate Conditioning. You've been . . . how can you . . . why don't the inhibitions . . ."

"Let me answer poor George's questions," said Saim. He slipped into Ancienglis, and the others stared at the fluidity with which he spoke. It wasn't like the thin Educator-veneer over Haribic at all.

"We don't know if it *was* started, George," said Saim. "The virus killed almost every adult. There was an immunity among children below the ages of 12-13-14. Below 12 the virus didn't strike. It took a few 13-year-olds, more 14-year-olds. Above 14 it took all but a small group of adults."

"You can't know this," protested ó Plar. "The last time, when you came out of the *kabah* . . ."

"Be quiet, *Uncle*," said Saim.

George said: "You spoke of some adults pulling through it. Why didn't they get it?"

"They were a sect of Buddhist monks in Arkansas. They'd built themselves a shelter. They expected a war and wanted to preserve their teachings for the survivors."

"You must not bring the names of the Eight Patriarch Bodhisattvas into this room!" protested ó Plar. Hé felt a giant outrage. *The violence! The defilement!*

"The Bodhisattvas," mused Saim. "Arthur Washington, Lincoln Howorth, Adoula Sampson, Samuael . . ."

"Saim, please!" begged ó Plar, and he stood there trembling between his human hope and his conditioned impulses.

Saim's voice softened. "It's all right, my friend. The dying days are gone. I'm just working myself up to it."

ó Plar closed his eyes, unable to act because that would require violence, but still impelled by *kabah* demands. The dangerous alternative was to resign himself to negative thought. He let the accident prayer well up into consciousness.

"But I was in a shelter," said George. "And I got this virus. How is that possible?"

"You probably had contact with people from the outside," said Saim. "Our Patriarchs didn't. They were in their shelter, breathing filtered air, when the virus came. They didn't even know of it. They stayed there, deep in contemplation until long after the virus was past. Thus did Lord Buddha preserve them. For when they emerged, there were only children in the world."

"Only children," murmured George. "Then my kids, and my wife, all . . ." He broke off, and for a long moment stared up at Saim. Presently, he said in a flat voice: "My world's gone, isn't it?"

"Gone," agreed Saim. "And while it had its share of mistakes, we made a bigger one."

ó Katje said: "Profanity!"

Saim ignored her. "There was an electronics specialist among our Patriarchs," he said. "He thought he could enforce peace for evermore. To do this, he built an instrument that shocks the primitive part of the human mind. The shocks revive terrors from the womb. With this you can introduce terrible enforcements for any behaviour desired. The staff you saw me break? That's a relatively mild form of this instrument. A reminder."

"What behaviour?" whispered George. He felt a sense of mounting horror at the logical projection of what Saim had said.

"Aversion to violence," said Saim. "That was the basic idea. It got out of hand for a stupidly simple reason that our Patriarch Samuael should have foreseen."

"Saim, Saim," whispered ó Plar. "I cannot hold out much longer."

"Patience," said Saim. He faced George. "Do you see it? Many things can be interpreted as violent: Surgery. Sex. Loud noises. Each year the list grows longer and the number of humans grows smaller. There are some the *kabah* tanks cannot revive. The flesh is there, but the will is gone."

ó Katje clasped her hands in front of her, said: "Saim, how can you do this terrible . . ."

"An accident," said Saim. "Eh, *Uncle*?" He glanced at the bowed head of ó Plar. "That's what you've hoped for, isn't it? Deep down where the *kabah* room never quite touches? Down where the little voices whisper and protest?"

"Accident," said Ren. "ó Katje said something about an accident."

"What's this about *kabah* room and accident?" demanded George. "What the hell's a *kabah*?"

Saim looked at the ceiling, then to the door on his right. Out there—the hall, another room, the control panel he'd seen George operating. His memory focused on a red handle. That'd be the one, of course. Even without George's example, he'd have known. His hands would have known what they had probed and studied to exhaustion.

"Won't anybody explain anything?" demanded George.

A few more moments won't matter, thought Saim. He said: "The *kabah* room? That's the great granddaddy of the staffs. That's the personality carver, the shaper, the twister, the . . ."

"Stop it!" screamed ó Katje.

"Help her, Ren," said Saim.

Ren shook himself out of his shock, moved to ó Katje's side.

"Don't touch me!" she hissed.

"You'll take a tranquillizer," said Saim.

It was a flat, no-nonsense command. She found herself taking a pill from Ren's palm, gulping it. The others waited for her to sink back against her chair.

Saim returned his attention to George. "I'm stalling, of course. I've a job to do."

"You'll do it?" whispered ó Plar.

"I'll do it."

George said: "This *kabah*, this instrument you . . ."

"Ultimate Conditioning," said Saim. "Priests and Priestesses must go through it each year. Renewal. If your unconscious protest at the way of things isn't too strong, you get some new personality carving, and you're sent out to live another year, and to herd the flock."

"Saim?" pleaded Jeni. "You *are* Saim, aren't you?"

"I'm Saim," he said, but he kept his attention on George. "So that's how it is, George. Each year the shepherds are re-examined for deviation from the non-violent norm. If you fail . . ." He hesitated. ". . . you lose all your memories, and you spend some time in a big *kabah* rejuvenation tank. When a doctor brings you out of the tank, you're farmed out and raised just like a child." He turned to ó Plar. "Isn't that right, *Uncle?*"

"Please, Saim?" begged ó Plar. "What you're doing to my inhi . . ."

"The explosion!" said Jeni. She rose half out of her chair. "When you died, and I made Ren steal a *kabah* tank to . . . That's what did it. We couldn't understand. For a time, you spoke like a Priest, and acted like a Priest and . . ."

"Then you went blank," said Ren. "And later, you were Saim again."

"Saim!" whispered Jeni. "You were a Priest who failed in the *kabah!*"

Again, Saim patted Jeni's shoulder. "Ren's tank renewed old patterns with the recent ones, but the *kabah* erasure of my memories was recent and strong. Ren contributed to this moment by not connecting the suppressors in the tank. I suspect he didn't know what they were."

"What could we have been thinking of?" whispered Ren. Shame and guilt were submerged in him, cowering behind a massive sense of horror. The fact that he knew this horror came from conditioning helped not at all. "Revive the science of the Elders? Revive violence?"

"I'm beginning to see it," mused George. "A thousand years of this? Christ!"

"What we overlooked when we built the first *kabah* rooms," said Saim. "This is a violent universe. It takes a certain amount of violence to survive in it. But the conditioning prevents violence according to increasingly limited interpretations. In ultimate silence, dropping a pin is violent. The more peaceful we became, the narrower became the interpretation of violence. But if you subtract all violence . . . that's death."

Again Saim patted Jeni's shoulder. "Well, I was hoping somewhat that George would . . . but, no, this is my job." He took a deep breath. "Yes. My job. I'd suggest you all stay down here under cover where you'll be safe from the Millennial Display. Soon, now, the *kabah* rooms will be gone."

ó Plar stood up, spoke slowly against his inhibitions: "You . . . are . . . going . . . to . . . explode . . . the . . . weapons?"

"I'm going to send them winging," said Saim. It was an almost non-committal statement in its tone.

"But all that death," whispered Jeni. "Saim, think of all the people who'll die!"

"That's all right," said Saim. "They've died before."

And he turned, walked towards the door into the hall. *My name is Samuael,* he thought. *Patriarch Samuael.*

THE PRIESTS OF PSI

The instant he stepped out of the transport's shields into Amel's sunlight warmth on the exit ramp Orne felt the surge of psi power around him. It was like being caught in a strange magnetic field. He caught the hand rail in sudden dizziness, stared down some two hundred metres at the glassy tricrete of the space port. Heatwaves shimmered off the glistening surface, baking the air even up to this height. There was no wind except inside him where the hidden gusts of the psi fields howled against his recently awakened senses.

The techs who had trained Orne in the use of the flesh-buried psi detection instruments had given him a small foretaste of this sensation back in the laboratory on Marak. It had been far short of this reality. The first sharp signal of the primary detector concealed in his neck had been replaced by the full spectrum of psi awareness.

Orne shuddered. Amel crawled with skin-creeping sensations. Weird urges flickered through his mind like flashes of heat lightning. He wanted to grunt like a wallowing *kiriffa*, and in the next instant felt laughter welling in him while a sob tore at his throat.

I knew it was going to be bad, he thought. *They warned me.*

The counter-conditioning only made this moment worse because now he was *aware*. Without the psi training, he knew that his mind would have confused the discrete sensations into a combined awe-fear—perfectly logical emotions for him to feel when debarking on the priest planet.

This was holy ground: sanctuary of all the religions in the known universe (and, some said, of all the religions in the *un*known universe).

Orne forced his attention on to the inner focus as the techs had taught him. Slowly, psi awareness dimmed to background annoyance. He drew in a deep breath of the hot, dry air. It was vaguely unsatisfying as though lacking some essential element to which his lungs were accustomed.

Still holding the rail, he waited to make certain he had subdued the ghost urges within him. Across the ramp, the glistening inner surface of the opened port reflected his image, distorting it slightly in a way that accented his differences from the lean, striding norm. He looked like a demigod reincarnated out of this world's ancient past: square and solid with the corded neck muscles of a heavy-grav native. A faint scar demarked the brow line of his close-cropped red hair. Other fine scars on his bulldog face were visible because he knew where to look, and his memory told of more scars on his heavy body. There was a half-humorous saying in Investigation & Adjustment that senior field agents could be detected by the number of scars and medical patches they carried.

Orne tugged at the black belt on his aqua toga, feeling uncomfortable in this garment that all "students" on Amel had to wear.

The yellow sun, Dubhe, hung at the meridian in a cloudless blue sky. It hammered through the toga with oppressive warmth. Orne felt the perspiration slick on his body. One step away the escalfield hummed softly, ready to drop him into the bustle visible at the foot of the transport. Priests and passengers were engaged in some kind of ceremony down there—initiation of the new students. Faintly to his ears came a throbbing drum-chant and a sing-song keening almost hidden beneath the port's machinery clatter.

Orne studied the scene around him, still waiting to make sure he would not betray his awareness. The transport's ramp commanded a sweeping view: a fantastic scratchwork of towers, belfries, steeples, monoliths, domes, ziggurats, pagodas, stupas, minarets, dagobas. They cluttered a flat plain that stretched to a horizon dancing in the heatwaves. Golden sunlight danced off bright primary colours and weathered pastels—buildings in tile and stone, tricrete and plasteel, and the synthetics of a thousand thousand civilizations.

Staring out at the religious warren, Orne experienced an abrupt feeling of dread at the unknown things that could be waiting in those narrow, twisted streets and jumbled buildings. The stories that leaked out of Amel always carried a hint of forbidden mystery, and Orne knew his emotions were bound to be tainted by some of that mystery. But his sudden dread shifted subtly to a special kind of fear.

This *peculiar* fear, coming out of his new awareness, had begun back on Marak.

Orne had been seated at the desk in his bachelor officer quarters, staring out at the park-like landscape of the I–A university grounds. Marak's green sun, low in the afternoon quadrant, had seemed distant and cold. Orne had been filling in as a lecturer on "Exotic Clues to War Tendencies" while waiting for his wedding to Diana Bullone. He was scheduled to marry the High Commissioner's daughter in only three weeks, and after a honeymoon on Kirachin he was expecting permanent assignment to the anti-war college. He could look forward to a life of training new I–A agents in the arts of seeking out and destroying the seeds that could grow into another Rim War.

That had been his concept of the future that afternoon on Marak. But suddenly he had turned away from his desk to frown at the stiffly regulation room. Something was awry. He studied the grey walls, the sharp angles of the bunk, the white bedcover with its blue I-A monogram: the crossed sword and stylus. The room's other chair stood backed against the foot of the bunk, leaving a three-centimetre clearance for the grey flatness of the closet door.

Something he could not define was making him restless—call it premonition.

Abruptly, the hall door banged open. Umbo Stetson,

Orne's superior officer, strode into the room. The section chief wore his characteristic patched blue fatigues. His only badge of rank, golden I–A emblems on his collar and uniform cap, looked faintly corroded. Orne wondered when they had last been polished, then pushed the thought aside. Stetson reserved all of his polish for his mind.

Behind the I–A officer rolled a mechanocart piled with cramtapes, microfilms and even some old-style books. It trundled itself into the room, its wheels rumbling as it cleared the doorsill. The door closed itself.

Good Lord! thought Orne. *Not an assignment! Not now.* He got to his feet, looked first at the cart, then at Stetson. There was an edge of uneasiness in Orne's voice as he asked: "What's this, Stet?"

Stetson pulled out the chair from the foot of the bunk, straddled it, sailed his cap on to the blanket. His dark hair straggled in an uncombed muss. His eyelids drooped, accenting his usual look of haughty superciliousness.

"You've had enough assignments to know what this is," he growled. A wry smile touched his lips. "Got a little job for you."

"Don't I have any say in this any more?" asked Orne.

"Well now, things may've changed a bit, and then again maybe they haven't," said Stetson.

"I'm getting married in three weeks," said Orne. "To the daughter of the High Commissioner."

"Your wedding is being postponed," said Stetson. He held up a hand as Orne's face darkened. "Wait a bit. Just postponed. Emergency. The High Commissioner sent his charming daughter off today on a job we just trumped up for the purpose."

Orne's voice was dangerously low: "What purpose?"

"The purpose of getting her out of your hair. You're leaving for Amel in six days and there's lots to be done before you're ready to go."

Orne drummed his fingers on the desk. "Just like that. Wedding's off. I'm assigned to a . . . Amel?"

"Yes."

"What is this, Stet? Amel's a picnic ground."

"Well . . ." Stetson shook his head. "Maybe not."

A sudden fear struck Orne. "Whose job was trumped up?" he demanded. "Has Diana . . ."

"She's off to Franchi Primus to help design a new uniform for the I–A women," said Stetson. "That safe enough for you?"

"But why so sudden?"

"We have to get you ready for Amel. Miss Bullone would have wasted time, diverted your attention. She knows something's up, but she takes orders just like the rest of us in the I–A. Have I made myself clear?"

"No notice. No nothing. Oh, this I–A is real fun! I must recommend it every time I find a young fellow looking for a job!"

"Mrs Bullone will bring a note from Diana tonight," said Stetson. "She's perfectly safe. You can get married when this is over."

"Provided the I-A doesn't dream up some new emergency for me!" barked Orne.

"You're the ones who took the I–A oath," said Stetson. "You knew when you took it that this sort of thing could happen."

"I'm going to rewrite the oath," said Orne. "To the words: *'I pledge my life and my sacred honour to seek out and destroy the seeds of war wherever they may be found'* let us add: *'and I will sacrifice anything and anybody in the process.'*"

"Not a bad addition," said Stetson. "Why don't you recommend it when you get back?"

"*If* I get back! What's the emergency this time?"

"This emergency came hunting for you specifically," said Stetson.

"How thoughtful of it."

"Your name's on the list for the latest *summoning* to Amel."

"A religious student? But I've never applied for . . ."

"But your name's on the list. Nice great big letters. List signed by the Halmyrach Abbod himself."

"There has to be a mistake. It's obviously a confusion of names with . . ."

"You've been specifically identified by family and current abode. No mistake."

Orne pushed himself away from the desk. "But there *has* to be! I tell you I've never applied for . . ." He broke off. "Anyway, what's the difference? The I–A couldn't be interested in Amel. Never been a war anywhere near the place. The big shots were always afraid of offending their gods."

Stetson pointed to the mechanocart. "I don't have much time for this briefing, so stop interrupting. You're going to need everything on this cart and more. You're going to the medics this evening for a quick-heal operation. Some very hush-hush . . ." He frowned, repeated himself: ". . . *very* hush-hush equipment's going to be hidden under your skin. Do you know anything about psi powers?"

The change of pace caused Orne to blink. He wet his lips with his tongue. "You mean like that fellow on Wessen who was supposed to be able to jump to any planet in the universe without a ship?"

"Something like that."

"Say, whatever happened to him? All the stories, then . . ."

"Maybe it was a fake," said Stetson. "Maybe it wasn't. We hope you can find out. Our techs will be showing you some psi equipment later. An amplifier . . ."

"But how does this connect with Amel?"

"You're going to tell us . . . we hope. You see, Lew, we just had the confirmation early this morning. At the next session of the Assembly there's going to be a motion to do away with the I–A, turn all of our functions over to Rediscovery & Re-education."

"Put us under Tyler Gemine? That political hack! Half our problems come from Rah & Rah stupidities! They've damn' near bumbled us into another Rim War a dozen times!''

"Mmmmm, hmmmmm," said Stetson. "And the next session of the Assembly is just over the horizon—five months."

"But . . . but a motion like that wouldn't stand a chance! It's asinine! I mean, look at the . . ."

"You'll be interested to know, Lew, that the pressure for this change comes from the priests of Amel. There does not seem to be any doubt that religious heat can put it over."

"Which sect of the priests?"

"All of them."

Orne shook his head. "But there are thousands of sects on Amel . . . millions, maybe. Under the Ecumenical Truce they . . ."

"All of them," repeated Stetson.

Orne frowned. "None of this fits. If the priests are gunning for us, why would they invite an I–A field agent on to their planet at the same time? That doesn't . . ."

"Exactly," said Stetson. "I'm sure you'll jump with joy when you learn that nobody—repeat: nobody!—has ever before been able to put an agent into Amel. Not the I–A. Not the old Marakian Secret Service. Not even the Nathians. All attempts have been met with polite ejection. No agent's ever gone farther than their landing field." Stetson got to his feet, glared down at Orne. "You'd better get started on this background material I brought. Your first session with the techs is tonight after the medics get through with you."

"What provision will there be for getting me off if Amel goes sour?" asked Orne.

"None."

Orne bounced to his feet. "None?"

"Our best information indicates that your training —they call it 'The Ordeal'—takes about six months. If there's no report from you within that limit, we'll make inquiries."

"Like: '*What've you done with the body?*' " snarled Orne. "Hell! There might not even be an I–A to make an inquiry in six months!"

Stetson shrugged. "I know this is sudden, and our data's skimpy where it . . ."

"This is like a last resort!"

"Exactly, Lew. But we have to find out why the galactic centre of all religions has turned against us. We have no hope of going in there and subduing them. It'd start religious uprisings all through the galaxy. Make the Rim War look like a game of ball at a girl's school. I'm not even certain we could get enough volunteers to do the job. We never qualify an agent because of his religion, but I'm damned sure they'd *qualify* us on that score. No. We have to find out why! Maybe we can change whatever's bothering them. It's our only hope. Maybe they don't understa . . ."

"What if they have plans for conquest by war? What then, Stet? A new faction could've come to power on Amel. Why not?"

Stetson looked sad, shrugged. "If you could prove it . . ." He shook his head.

"When am I going to the medics?"

"They'll come for you."

"Yeah. Somebody already came for me . . . it looks like."

It was early evening in Orne's hospital room at the I–A medical centre—the quiet time between dinner and visiting hours. The nurse had turned on the light beside his bed. It cast a soothing reflection from the green walls. The induction bandage felt bulky under his chin, but the characteristic quick-heal itching had not yet started.

Being in a hospital room made him vaguely uneasy. He knew why: the smells and the sounds reminded him of all the months he'd spent creeping back from death after his injuries in the Heleb uprising. Heleb had been another planet where war just could *not* start. Like Amel.

The door to his hospital room opened. A tech officer

strode through, closed the door. The man's uniform bore odd forked lightning insignia. Orne had never seen the emblem before. *Psi?* he wondered. The officer stopped at the foot of the bed, leaned on the cross-bar. His face was bird-like. There was a long nose, pointed chin, narrow mouth. The eyes made quick, darting movements. He was tall, bone skinny, and when he lifted his right hand in a mock salute, the gesture was fluttery.

"Hi," he said. "I'm Ag Emolirdo, head of our Psi Section. The Ag is for Agony."

Unable to move his head because of the induction bandage, Orne stared down the length of the bed at Emolirdo. The officer carried an aura of . . . confidence, *knowing* confidence. He reminded Orne of a priest back on Chargon. This idea made Orne uneasy. He said: "How d'you do."

"This will have to move rather rapidly," said the tech. He smiled. "You'll be into parahypnoid sessions by midnight."

"Join the I–A and learn the mysteries of the universe," Orne said.

Emolirdo cocked one eyebrow. "Were you aware that you're a psi focus?"

"A what?" Orne tried to sit up, but the bandage restraints held him fast.

"Psi focus," said Emolirdo. "You'll understand it later. Briefly, you're an island of order in a disordered universe. Four times since you came to the attention of the I–A you've done the impossible. Any one of the incidents you tackled should have led to ferment and then general war. You've brought order out of . . ."

"So I did what I was trained to do."

"Trained? By whom?"

"By my government . . . by the I–A. That's a stupid question."

"Is it?" Emolirdo found a chair, sat down, his head level with Orne's. "Well, we won't argue the point. The chief thing now is that you know consciously the broad areas to be covered. You understand?"

"I know the parahypnoid technique," said Orne.

"First, psi focus," said Emolirdo. "Let us define life as a bridge between Order and Chaos. Then, let us define Chaos as raw energy available to anything that can subdue it—that is, to anything that can put it into some order. Life, then, becomes stored Chaos. You follow?"

"I hear you. Get on with it."

"Ah impatience of the non-adept," murmured Emolirdo. He cleared his throat. "To restate the situation, Life feeds on Chaos, but must exist in Order. An apparent paradox. This brings us to the condition called *stasis*. Stasis is like a magnet. It attracts free energy to itself until the pressure of Chaos becomes too great and it explodes . . . and, exploding, goes back to Chaos. One is left with the unavoidable conclusion that Stasis leads always to Chaos."

"That's dandy," said Orne.

Emolirdo frowned. "This rule is true on both the levels of chemical-inanimate and chemical-animate, Mr Orne. For example, ice, the stasis of water, explodes when brought into abrupt contact with extreme heat. The frozen society explodes when exposed suddenly to the chaos of war or the *apparent* chaos of a strange new society. Nature abhors stasis."

"Like a vacuum," said Orne.

"Precisely."

"Outside of the vacuum in my head, what other little problems do we have?" asked Orne.

"Amel."

"Oh, yes. Another vacuum?"

"Apparently a stasis that does not explode."

"Then maybe it isn't static."

"You're very astute, Mr Orne."

"Golly . . . thanks."

"You think you're being very humorous, don't you, Mr Orne?"

"I thought you were the prize joker here. What's all this have to do with Amel?"

"Miracles," said Emolirdo. "You obviously were summoned to Amel because they consider you a worker of miracles."

Pain stabbed through Orne's bandaged neck as he tried to turn his head. "Miracles?" he croaked.

"Substitute *psi* for miracle," said the tech. "*Psi focus,* to be more precise." A weird half smile flickered across Emolirdo's mouth. It was as though he had fought down an internal dispute on whether to laugh or cry, solved it by doing neither.

Orne felt confused, uneasy. He said: "You've left me."

"Psi focus is the scientific label for miracle," said Emolirdo. "It's something that happens outside of recognized channels, in spite of accepted rules. Religions say it's a miracle. Certain scientists say. we have encountered a psi focus. That can be either a person or a locale."

"I'm not reading you at all," muttered Orne.

"You've heard of the ancient miracle caverns on the older planets?"

Orne blinked. "I've heard the legends."

"We're convinced that they concealed shapes . . . convolutions that projected out of our apparent universe. Except at these focus points, the raw energy of outer Chaos cannot be bent to our needs. But *at* these focus points, Chaos—the wild energy—is richly available in a way that can be tamed. It may be moulded in unique ways that defy ordinary rules." Emolirdo's eyes blazed. He seemed to be fighting a great inner excitement.

Orne wet his lips. "Shapes?"

"Men have bent wires, coiled them, carved bits of plastic, jumbled together odd assortments of apparently unrelated objects. And weird things happen. A smooth piece of metal becomes tacky, as though you'd smeared it with glue. A man draws a pentagram on a certain floor, and flame dances within it. Smoke curls from a strangely shaped bottle and does another man's bidding, obeys his will. Then there are certain men who conceal this focus within themselves. They walk into . . . nothing, and reappear light years away. They look at a person suffering from an incurable disease. The incurable is cured. They raise the dead. They read minds."

Orne tried to swallow in a dry throat. "All this is psi?"

"We believe so." Emolirdo bent towards Orne's bedside light, thrust a fist in between the light and the green wall. "Look at the wall."

"I can't turn my head," said Orne.

"Sorry. Just a shadow." Emolirdo withdrew his hand. "But let us say there were sentient beings confined to the flat plane of that wall. Let us say they saw the shadow of my fist. Could a genius among them imagine the shape that cast the shadow—a shape that projected outside of his dimensions?"

"Good question," said Orne.

"What if the being in the wall fashioned a device that projected into our dimension?" asked Emolirdo. "He would be like the blind men studying the legendary elephant. His device would respond in ways that do not fit his dimension. He would have to set up all kinds of new postulates."

Under the bandage, the skin of Orne's neck began to itch maddeningly. He resisted the desire to probe there with a finger. Bits of folklore from Chargon flitted through his memory: the magicians, the little people who granted wishes in a way that made the wisher regret his desires, the cavern where the sick were cured. The quick-heal itching lured his finger with almost irresistible force. He groped for a pill on his bedstand, gulped it down, waited for the relief.

Presently, Orne said: "What's this thing you've put in my neck?"

"It has a dual purpose," said Emolirdo. "It signals the presence of psi activity—psi *fields*, we call them. And it's an amplifier, giving a boost to any latent . . . ah, talents you may have. It'll often permit a novice to produce some of the minor psi effects.''

Orne rubbed the outside of his neck bandage, forced his hand away. "Such as what?''

"Oh . . . resisting psi-induced emotions, detecting motivation in others through some of their emotions. It may give a small degree of prescience. You'd be able to detect extremes of personal danger when they were still some distance off in time. You'll understand about this, after the parahypnoid session.''

Orne felt something tingling in his neck. There was a vacant sensation in the pit of his stomach. "Prescience?''

"You'd recognize it at first as a kind of fear . . . a *peculiar* kind of fear. Sometimes it's like hunger even though you've just eaten. Something feels like it's lacking . . . inside you, or in the air you breathe. If you feel it, you'll recognize it. It'll always be a warning of danger. Very trustworthy.''

Orne's skin felt clammy. There was the vacant sensation in his stomach. The air of the room felt stale. His immediate reaction was to reject the sensations and all of the suggestive conversation, but there was still the fact of Stetson. Nobody in the I–A was more coldly objective or quicker to toss out mumbo-jumbo. And Stetson obviously accepted this psi thing. Stetson could be trusted. That was the major fact keeping Orne from booting this . . . this . . .

"You look a little pale,'' said Emolirdo.

"Probably.'' Orne managed a tight smile. "I think I feel your prescience thing right now.''

"Describe your sensations.''

Orne obeyed.

"You feel irritated, jumpy without apparent reason,'' said Emolirdo. "Odd that it should happen so soon, before the training, that is. Unless . . .'' He pursed his lips.

"Unless what?''

"Unless your talent . . . were quite strong. And unless psi training itself were actually dangerous to you. Wouldn't that be interesting, though?''

"Yeah. Fascinating. I can hardly wait to get through this training and be on my way to Amel."

It was reluctance, Orne decided. There was no real excuse to wait up here on the transport's ramp any longer. Obviously, he had overcome the first staggering impact of the psi fields of Amel. There was still the prescient awareness of danger—like a sore tooth signalling its presence. The day was hot, and the toga was too heavy. He was soaked in perspiration.

Damn! If I wait too long they'll get suspicious.

He took a half step towards the escalfield, still fighting the reluctance. His nostrils caught an acrid bite of incense that had evaded the oil-and-ozone dominance of the landing area. In spite of counter-conditioning and carefully nurtured agnosticism, he felt an abrupt sensation of awe. Amel exuded an aura of magic that defied cynical disbelief.

The chanting and keening that lifted fog-like from the religious warren sparked memory fragments. Shards of his childhood on Chargon tumbled through Orne's mind: *the religious processions on holy days . . . the image of Mahmud glowering down from the* kiblah *. . . and the* azan *ringing out across the great square on the day of* Bairam—

"Let no blasphemy occur nor permit a blasphemer to live! May such a one be accursed of God and of the blessed from the sole of his foot to the crown of his head, sleeping and waking, sitting and standing . . ."

Orne shook his head.

Yes, bow down to Ullun, the star wanderer of the Ayrbs, he thought. Now would be a great time for him to get religion!

But the roots were deep. He tightened the belt of his toga, strode forward into the escalfield. Its feathery touch dropped him to the ground, disgorged him beside a covered walkway. A cluster of priests and students were pressed into the thin shade of the cover. They began to separate as Orne approached, leaving in pairs—a white-clad priest with each student.

One priest remained facing Orne. He was tall and with a thick body. There was a heavy feeling about him as though the ground would shudder when he walked. His head was shaved bald. Deep lines scratched patterns on his wide jowled face. Dark eyes glowered from beneath overhanging grey brows.

"Are you Orne?" the priest rumbled.

Orne stepped under the walkway. "That's right." There was a yellowish gleam to the priest's skin.

"I am Bakrish," said the priest. He put his slab hands on his hips, glared at Orne. "You missed the ceremony of lustration."

Something about the heavy figure, the glowering face reminded Orne abruptly of an I–A gunnery sergeant he had known. The thought restored Orne's sense of balance, brought a grin to his face.

"Sorry," said Orne. "I was enjoying the view."

"You find something amusing?" demanded Bakrish.

"This humble face reflects happiness," said Orne. "Happiness to be on Amel."

"Oh. Well, come along." Bakrish turned away, strode off under the covered walk, not looking to see if Orne followed.

Orne shrugged, set off after the priest, found that he had to force himself to a half trot to keep up with the other's long-legged stride.

No moving walks, no hopalongs, thought Orne. *This place is primitive.*

The walk jutted like a long beak from a windowless, low stone building. Double doors opened into a dim hall. The doors had to be opened manually, and one of them creaked. Bakrish led the way past rows of narrow cells open to the hall, came finally to another door. It opened into a cell slightly larger than the others, big enough to accommodate one small desk and two chairs. Pink light filled the room from concealed exciters.

Bakrish crossed the cell ahead of Orne, crunched into the chair behind the desk, motioned for Orne to take the other seat. "Sit down."

Orne complied, but with a sudden feeling of wariness.

Something here failed to add up for his highly tuned senses.

"As you know, we here on Amel live under the Ecumenical Truce," said Bakrish. "Your intelligence service will have briefed you on some of the significance behind that fact, of course."

Orne concealed his surprise at this turn in the conversation. He nodded.

Bakrish smiled. "The main thing you need to understand about it now is that there is nothing unusual in my being assigned as your guru."

"I *don't* understand."

"You are a follower of Mahmud. I am a Hynd and a *Wali*, under divine protection. Under the Truce, all of us serve the one God who has many names. You understand?"

"I see."

Bakrish nodded. "When Emolirdo told us about you, we had to see for ourselves, of course. That is why you are here."

Emolirdo a traitor! Iron control kept Orne from revealing his shock.

"You pose a fascinating problem," said Bakrish.

Anger coursed through Orne. *What a foul-up!* He set his face in a wolfish grin, probed with his newly awakened psi awareness for some weakness here, an emotion, a clue to the feeling of oddness about the room. "I'm so happy you've found something to keep you occupied," he said.

Bakrish leaned forward, glanced behind Orne, nodded. In the same instant, Orne felt the sensation of oddness dissipate. He whirled, caught a flicker of robe and a wheeled object being pulled away from the open door.

"That's better," said Bakrish. "Now we have the tensor phase pattern of your equipment. We can nullify it at will, or destroy you with it."

Orne froze. *What kind of a bomb did Emolirdo have the medics plant in me?*

"However, we do not wish to destroy you," said Bakrish. "For the time being we will not tamper with your equipment. We *want* you to use it."

Orne took two deep breaths. Without volition, his psi training took over. He concentrated on the inner focus for calmness. It came like a wash of cool water: icy, observant calm.

Boxed! All it took was one traitor! The thoughts blazed through his mind. But outwardly he remained calm, alert.

"Have you nothing to say?" asked Bakrish.

"Yes." Orne cleared his throat. "I want to see the Halmyrach Abbod. I've got to find out why you're trying to destroy the . . ."

"All in due time," said Bakrish.

"Where's the Abbod?"

"Nearby. When the time comes for you to have your audience with him it will be arranged."

"Meanwhile, I just wait for you to blow me up!"

"Blow you . . ." Bakrish looked puzzled. "Believe me, my young friend, we have no desire to cause your destruction. That is merely a necessary precaution. Now, there are two facts here: You want to find out about us, and we want to find out about you. The best way for both of us to accomplish our aims would be for you to submit to your ordeal. You really don't have any choice, of course."

"You mean I let you lead me around like a *grifka* being brought to the slaughterhouse! Either that or else you destroy me."

"It would be better if you just looked on this as an interesting test," murmured Bakrish. "Your bloody thoughts really aren't suitable."

"Somehow, I'm going to find out what makes you tick," grated Orne. "When I do, I'm going to smash your mainspring!"

Bakrish frowned, swallowed. "You *must* be exposed to the holy mysteries," he said. His yellow skin paled.

Orne leaned back. His sudden burst of bravado had left an aftermath of embarrassment. He thought: *This joker should've laughed at me. He's in the driver's seat. But my threat frightened him. Why?*

"Do you submit to your ordeal?" asked Bakrish.

Orne pushed himself up out of the chair. "You said it for me: I really don't have any choice."

"This is the cell of meditation-on-faith," said Bakrish. "Stretch out on the floor, flat on your back. Do not try to sit up or stand until I give you permission. It is very dangerous."

"Why?" Orne looked around the room. It was high and narrow. Walls, floor and ceiling looked like white stone veined by thin brown lines like insect tracks. Pale white light, sourceless and as flat as skimmed milk, filled the room. A damp stone smell permeated the place.

"Flat on your back you are relatively safe," said Bakrish. "Accept my word for it. I have seen the results of disbelief."

Orne cleared his throat, feeling suddenly cold. He sat down, stretched out on the floor. The stone was chill against his back.

"Once started on your ordeal, the only way out is to go through it," said Bakrish.

"Have *you* been through this?" asked Orne.

"But of course."

Orne probed for the other's motive-emotions, met a sense of cold sympathy . . . if the psi awareness could be trusted. After all, much of it had come from Emolirdo, a traitor.

"So I've crawled into your tunnel . . . or is it a cave?" said Orne. "What's at the other end?"

"That's for you to discover."

"You're using me to find out something, Bakrish. What if I refuse to co-operate? Is that stalemate?"

A sense of tentative regret radiated from Bakrish. "When the scientist sees that his experiment has failed, he is not necessarily barred from further experiments . . . with new equipment. You truly have no choice."

"Then let's get on with it."

"As you will." Bakrish moved to the end wall. It swung open to reveal the outer hallway, closed behind the priest. There was an abrupt feeling of increased pressure.

Orne studied the cell. It appeared to be about four metres long, two metres wide, some ten metres high. But the mottled stone ceiling appeared blurred. Perhaps the room was higher. The pale lighting could be designed for confusing the senses. He probed the prescient sense, felt its amorphous twinge—peril.

The priest's voice suddenly filled the room, booming from a concealed speaker: "You are enclosed within a psi machine. This ordeal is ancient and exacting: to test the quality of your faith. Failure means loss of your life, your soul or both."

Orne clenched his hands. Perspiration made his palms oily. An abrupt increase in background psi activity registered on his booster.

"Immerse yourself in the mystical stream," said Bakrish. "Of what are you afraid?"

Orne thought of the pressures focused on him, all the evidence of deep and hidden intent. "I don't like to act just on faith. I like to know where I'm going."

"Sometimes you must go for the sake of going," said Bakrish. "In fact, you do this all the time when . . ."

"Nuts!"

"When you press the stud to turn on a room's lights, you act on faith that there will be light," said Bakrish.

"Faith in past experience."

"And what about the first time?"

"I guess I must've been surprised at the light."

"Then prepare yourself for surprises, because there is no lighting mechanism in your cell. The light you see there exists because you desire it, and for no other reason."

"What . . ."

Darkness engulfed the room.

Bakrish's voice filled the darkness with a husky whisper. "Have faith."

The prescient warning gripped Orne: writhing terror. He fought down the desire to jump up and dash for the door wall. The priest's warning, grimly matter of fact, had rung true. Death lay in flight.

Smoky glowing appeared near the ceiling, coiled down towards Orne.

Light?

Orne lifted his right hand. He couldn't see the hand. The radiance cast no light into the rest of the cell. The sense of pressure in the cell increased with each heartbeat.

Light if I wish it? Well . . . it became dark when I doubted.

He thought of the milky light.

Shadowless illumination flickered into being, but near the ceiling where he had seen the glowing radiance there boiled a black cloud. It beckoned like the outer darkness of space.

Orne froze, staring.

Darkness filled the room.

Again, radiance glowed at the ceiling.

The klaxon of prescient fear cried through Orne. He closed his eyes in the effort of concentration. Immediately, fear lessened. His eyes snapped open in shock.

Fear!

And the ghostly glowing crawled nearer.

Eyes closed.

Still the sense of peril, but without immediacy.

Fear equals darkness. Even in the light, darkness beckons. He stilled his breathing, concentrated on the inner focus. *Faith?* Blind *faith? What do they want of me? Fear brings the dark.*

He forced his eyes to open, stared into the lightless void of the cell. Radiance coiling downwards. *Even in the darkness there is light. But it's not really light because I can't see by it.*

It was like a time he could remember—long ago in childhood: darkness in his own bedroom. Mooncast shadows transmuted to monsters. He had clenched his eyes tightly closed, fearful that if he opened them he would see a thing too horrible to face.

Orne stared up at the coiling radiance. *False light. Like false hope.* The radiance coiled backwards into itself, receding. *Utter darkness equals utter fear.*

The radiance winked out.

Dank, stone-smelling darkness permeated the cell, a

darkness infected with creeping sounds—claw scrabbles and hisses, little slitherings . . .

Orne invested the sounds with every shape of terror his imagination could produce: poisonous lizards, insane monsters . . . The peril sense enfolded him, and he hung there suspended in it.

Bakrish's hoarse whisper snaked through the darkness: "Orne? Are your eyes open?"

His lips trembled with the effort to speak: "Yes."

"What do you *see*, Orne?"

An image suddenly danced on to the black field in front of Orne: Bakrish in an eerie red light, leaping and capering, grimacing . . .

"What do you see?" hissed Bakrish.

"You. I see you in Sadun's inferno."

"The hell of Mahmud?"

"Yes. Why?"

"Orne, do you not prefer the light?"

"Why do I see you?"

"Orne, I *beg* of you! Choose the . . ."

"*Why* do I see you in . . ." Orne broke off. He had the feeling that something peered inside him with heavy deliberation, checked his thoughts, his vital processes, weighed them. He knew suddenly that if he willed it, Bakrish would be cast into the deepest torture pit dreamed of in Mahmud's nightmares. *Why not? Then again: why? Who am I to decide? He may not be the right one. Perhaps the Halmyrach Abbod . . .*

Groaning, creaking filled the stones of the cell. A tongue of flame lanced out of the darkness above Orne, poised. It cast a ruddy glow on the stone walls.

Prescient fear clawed at him.

Faith? He had the inner knowledge—not faith—that in this instant he could do a dangerous and devilish thing: cast a man into eternal torture. *Which man and why? No man.* He rejected the choice.

Above him, the dancing flame receded, winked out, leaving only darkness and its slithering noises. Realization swept over Orne: he felt his own fingernails trembling and scrabbling against the stone floor—*claws!* He laughed aloud, stilled his hands. The claw sound stopped. He felt his feet writhing with involuntary efforts at flight. He stilled his feet, recognized the absence of the suggestive slithering. And the hissing! He focused on it, realized that it was his own breath fighting through clenched teeth.

Orne laughed.

Light?

In sudden perversity, he rejected the idea of light. Somehow, he knew this machine was responding to his innermost wishes, but only to those wishes uncensored by a doubting consciousness. Light was his for the willing of it, but he chose the darkness, and in the sudden release of tension, ignored Bakrish's warning, got to his feet. He smiled into the darkness, said: "Open the door, Bakrish."

Again, Orne felt something peer inside him, and recognized it for a psi probe—greatly magnified from the training probe used by Emolirdo. Someone was checking his motives.

"I'm not afraid," said Orne. "Open the door."

A scraping sound grated in the cell. Light fanned inwards from the hall as the end wall swung open. Orne looked out at Bakrish, a shadow framed against the light like a robed statue.

The Hynd stepped forwards, jerked to a halt as he saw Orne standing.

"Did you not prefer the light, Orne?"

"No."

"But you must have understood this test: you're standing . . . unafraid of my warning."

"This machine obeys my uncensored will," said Orne. "That's faith: the uncensored will."

"You *do* understand. And still you preferred the dark?"

"Does that bother you, Bakrish?"

"Yes, it does."

"Good."

"I see." Bakrish bowed. "Thank you for sparing me."

"You know about that?"

"I felt flames and heat, smelled the burning . . ." The priest shook his head. "The life of a guru here is not safe. Too many possibilities."

"You were safe," said Orne. "I censored my will."

"The most enlightened degree of faith," murmured Bakrish.

"Is that all there is to my ordeal?" Orne glanced around at the darkened cell walls.

"Merely the first step," said Bakrish. "There are seven steps in all: the test of faith, the test of the miracle's two faces, the test of dogma and ceremony, the test of ethics, the test of the religious ideal, the test of service to life, and the test of the mystical experience. They do not necessarily fall in that order."

Orne felt the absence of immediate prescient fear. He tasted a sense of exhilaration. "Then let's get on with it."

Bakrish sighed. "Holy Empress defend me," he muttered, then: "Yes, of course. Your next step: the miracle's two faces."

And the prescient sense of peril began to flicker within Orne. Angrily, he put it aside. *I have faith,* he thought. *Faith in myself. I've proved I can conquer my fear.*

"Well, what're we waiting for?" he demanded.

"Come along," said Bakrish. He turned with a swirl of his white robe, led the way down the hall.

Orne followed. "By miracle, do you mean psi focus?"

"What difference does it make what we call it?" asked Bakrish.

"If I solve all your riddles, do you take the heat off the I–A?" asked Orne.

"The heat . . . Oh, you mean . . . That is a question for the Halmyrach Abbod to decide."

"He's nearby, eh?"

"Very near."

Bakrish stopped before a heavy bronze door at the end of the hall, turned an ornate handle at one side, threw his shoulder against the door. It creaked open. "We generally don't come this way," he said. "These two tests seldom follow each other."

Orne blinked, followed the priest through the door into a gigantic round room. Stone walls curved away to a domed ceiling far above them. In the high curve of the ceiling slit windows admitted thin shafts of light that glittered downwards through gilt dust. Orne followed the light downwards to its focus on a straight barrier wall about twenty metres high and forty or fifty metres long, chopped off and looking incomplete in the middle of the room. The wall was dwarfed in the immensity of the domed space.

Bakrish circled around behind Orne, swung the heavy door closed, nodded towards the central barrier. "We go over there." He led the way.

Their slapping footsteps echoed off the walls. The damp stone smell was strong, like a bitter taste. Orne glanced left, saw doors evenly spaced around the room's perimeter, bronze doors like the one they had entered.

As they approached the barrier, Orne centred his attention on it. The surface looked to be a smooth grey plastic—featureless, but somehow menacing.

Bakrish stopped about ten metres from the middle of the wall. Orne stopped beside him, became conscious of prescient fear: something to do with the wall. Within him there was a surging and receding like waves on a beach. Emolirdo had described this sensation and interpreted it: *Infinite possibilities in a situation basically perilous.*

A blank wall?

"Orne, is it not true that a man should obey the orders of his superiors?" Bakrish's voice carried a hollow echo in the immensity of the room.

Orne's throat felt dry. He cleared it, rasped: "I suppose so . . . if the orders make sense. Why?"

"You were sent here as a spy, Orne. By rights, anything that happens to you is no concern of ours."

Orne tensed. "What're you driving at?"

Bakrish looked down at Orne, large eyes dark and glistening. "Sometimes these machines frighten us. Their methods are so unpredictable, and anyone who comes within the field of one of them can be subjected to its power."

"Like back there in that cell when you hung at the edge of the inferno?"

Bakrish shuddered. "Yes."

"But I still have to go through with this thing?"

"You must. It is the only way you will accomplish what you were sent here to do . . . and . . . you could not stop now, anyway. The ball is rolling down the hill. You don't even want to stop."

Orne tested this against his own feelings, shrugged. "I *am* curious."

"The thing is, Orne, you suspect us and fear us. These lead to hate. We saw that back there at the cell. But hate can be supremely dangerous to you in this present test. You . . ."

A scraping sound behing them brought Orne's attention around. Two oblate brothers deposited a heavy, square-armed chair on the stone floor facing the wall. They cast frightened glances at Orne, the wall, turned and scampered towards one of the heavy bronze doors.

"As I was saying, Orne, I am merely following orders here. I beg of you not to hate me, nor to hate anyone. You should not harbour hate during this test."

"What frightened those two fellows who brought that chair?" asked Orne. He watched the pair scurry through their door, slam it behind them.

"They know the reputation of this test. The very fabric of our universe is woven into it. Many things can hang in the balance here. Infinite possibilities."

Cautiously, Orne probed for Bakrish's motives. The priest obviously sensed the probe. He said: "I am afraid, Orne. Is that what you wanted to know?"

"Why are you afraid?"

"In *my* ordeal, this test proved nearly fatal. I had sequestered a core of hate. This place clutches at me even now." He shivered.

Orne found the priest's fright unsteadying. He looked at the chair. It was squat, ugly. An inverted metallic bowl projected on an arm over the seat. "What's the chair?"

"You must sit down in it."

Orne glanced at the grey wall, at Bakrish, back to the chair. There was tension here as though each heartbeat pumped pressure into the room. The surging and receding of his prescient sense increased, but he felt himself committed to this blind course.

"Sometimes we must go for the sake of going." The words rang in his memory. Who had said them?

He crossed to the chair, turned, sat down. In the act of sitting, the prescient sense of peril came to full surge, stayed. But there was no time for a change of heart. Metal bands leaped from concealed openings in the chair, pinned his arms, circled his chest and legs. Orne surged against them, twisting.

"Do not struggle," warned Bakrish. "You cannot escape."

Orne sank back.

"Please, Orne: you must not hate us. Your danger is magnified manyfold if you do. Hate could make you fail."

"Dragging you down with me, eh?"

"Quite possibly," muttered Bakrish. "One never quite escapes the consequences of one's hate." He stepped behind the chair, lowered the inverted bowl over Orne's head. "If you move suddenly or try to jerk away the microfilament probes within this bowl will cause you great pain."

Orne felt something touch his scalp, crawling, tickling. "What is this?"

"One of the great psi machines." Bakrish adjusted something on the chair. Metal clicked. "Observe the wall. It can manifest your most latent urges. You can bring about miracles, call forth the dead, do many wonders. You may be on the brink of a deep mystical experience."

Orne swallowed in a dry throat. "You mean if I wanted my father to appear here he would?"

"He is deceased?"

"Yes."

"Then it could happen. But I must caution you. The things you see here will not be hallucination. And one thing more: If you are successful in calling forth the dead, you must realize that what you call forth will be that dead person, and yet not that dead person."

The back of Orne's right arm itched. He longed to scratch it. "How can . . ."

"The paradox is like this: any living creature manifested here through your will must be invested with your psyche as well as its own. Its matter will impinge on your matter. All of your memories will be available to whatever living flesh you call forth."

"But . . ."

"Hear me out, Orne. In some cases, your *creates* may fully understand their duality. Others will reject your half out of hand because they have not the capacity. Some may even lack sentience."

Orne felt the fear driving Bakrish's words, sensed truth in them. *He believes this, anyway.* He said: "But why trap me here in this chair?"

"It's important that you do not run away from yourself." Bakrish's hand fell on Orne's shoulder. "I must leave you now. May grace guide you."

There was a swishing of robes as the priest strode away. Presently a door closed, its sound a hollow sharpness. Orne felt infinitely alone.

A faint humming became audible—distant bee sound. The booster in his neck tugged sharply, and he felt the flare of a psi field around him. The barrier wall blinked alive to the colour of grass green, and immediately began to crawl with iridescent purple lines. They squirmed and writhed like countless glowing worms trapped in a viscid green aquarium.

Orne drew in a shuddering breath. Prescient fear hammered at him. The crawling purple lines held hypnotic fascination. Some appeared to waft out towards him. The shape of Diana's face glowed momentarily among them. He tried to hold the image, saw it melt away.

Because she's alive? he wondered.

Shapeless deformities squirmed across the wall, coalesced abruptly into the outline of a *shriggar*, the saw-toothed lizard that Chargonian mothers invoked to frighten their children into obedience. The image took on more substance, developed yellow scale plates, stalk eyes.

Time suddenly slowed to a grinding, creeping pace within Orne. He thought back to his childhood on Chargon: terror memories.

But even then shriggar were extinct, he told himself.

Memory persisted down a long corridor full of empty echoes that suggested gibbering insanity. Down . . . down . . . down . . . He remembered childish laughter, a kitchen, his mother. And there were his sisters screaming derisively. And he remembered himself cowering, ashamed. He couldn't have been more than three years old. He had come running into the house to babble that he had seen a *shriggar* . . . in the deep shadows of the creek gully.

Laughing girls! Hateful little girls! "*He thinks he saw a shriggar!*" "*Hush now, you two.*"

On the green wall, the *shriggar* outline bulged outwards. A taloned foot extended. It stepped from the wall on to the stone floor: half again as tall as a man, stalked eyes swivelling right, left . . .

Orne jerked out of his reverie, felt painful throbbing as his head movement disturbed the microfilament probes.

There was scratching of talons on stone as the *shriggar* took three tentative steps away from the wall. Orne tasted the fear within himself, thought: *Some ancestor of mine was hunted by such a creature! The panic goes too deep!* It was a clear thought that flickered through his mind while every sense remained focused on the nightmare lizard.

Its yellow scales rasped with every breath it took. The narrow, birdlike head twisted to one side, lowered. Its beak mouth opened to reveal a forked tongue and saw teeth.

Primordial instinct pressed Orne back in his chair. He smelled the stink of the creature: sickly sweet with overtones of sour cheese.

The *shriggar* bobbed its head, coughed: *"Chunk!"* Its stalk eyes moved, centred on Orne. One taloned foot lifted and it plunged into motion towards the figure trapped in the chair. Its high-stepping lope stopped about four metres away, and the lizard cocked its head to one side while it examined Orne.

He stared up at it, his only bodily sensation a vague awareness of tightness across chest and stomach. The beast stink was almost overpowering.

Behind the *shriggar*, the green wall continued to wriggle with iridescent purple lines. It was a background blur on Orne's eyes. The lizard moved closer, and he smelled a draught of breath as fetid as swamp ooze.

No matter what Bakrish said, this has to be hallucination, he told himself. *Shriggar have been extinct for centuries.* But another thought blinked at him: *The priests could have bred zoo specimens to maintain the species. How does anyone know what's been done here in the name of religion?*

The *shriggar* cocked its head to the other side.

At the green wall, lines solidified. Two children dressed in scanty sun aprons skipped out on to the stone floor. Their footsteps echoed, and childish giggling echoed in the vast emptiness. One child appeared to be about five years old, the other slightly older—possibly eight. The older child carried a small bucket with a toy shovel protruding from it. They stopped, looked around, confused.

The *shriggar* turned its head, bent its stalk eyes towards them. It swivelled its body back towards the wall, poised one foot, lunged into its high-stepping lope.

The youngest child looked up, squealed.

The *shriggar* increased its speed.

Shocked, Orne recognized the children: his two sisters, the ones who had laughed at his fearful cries on that long ago day. It was as though he had brought this incident to life for the sole purpose of venting his hate, inflicting on those children the thing they had derided.

The lizard swooped down, blocked the children from view. Orne tried to close his eyes, could not. There came a shriek cut off with abrupt finality. Unable to stop, the *shriggar* hit the green wall, *melted into it!*

The older child lay sprawled on the floor still clutching her bucket and toy shovel. A red smear spread across the stones beside her. She stared across the room at Orne, slowly got to her feet.

No matter what Bakrish said, this can't be real, thought Orne. Yet he felt an odd wash of relief that the *shriggar* had vanished.

The child began walking towards Orne, swinging her bucket. Her right hand clutched the toy shovel. She stared fixedly at Orne. He brought her name into his mind: *Maddie, my sister, Lurie. But she's a grown woman now, married and with children of her own.*

Flecks of sand marked the child's legs and cheeks. One of her two blonde braids hung down partly undone. She looked angry, shivering with an eight-year-old's fury. About two metres away she stopped.

"You did that!" she screamed.

Orne shuddered at the madness in the child voice. She lifted the bucket, hurled its contents at him. He shut his eyes, felt coarse sand deluge his face, pelt the silver dome, run down his cheeks. Pain coursed through him as he shook his head, disrupting the microfilaments against his scalp. Through slitted eyes he saw the dancing lines on the green wall leap into wild motion—bending, twisting, flinging. Orne stared at the purple frenzy through a red haze of pain. And he remembered the guru's warning that any life he called forth here would contain his own psyche as well as its own.

"Lurie," he said, "please try to . . ."

"You tried to get into my head!" she screamed. "But I pushed you out!"

Bakrish had said it: *"Others will reject your half out of hand because they have not the capacity."* This dual create had rejected him because her eight-year-old mind could not accept such an experience. And Orne realized that he was taking this scene as reality and not as hallucination.

"I'm going to kill you!" screamed Lurie.

She hurled herself at him, the toy shovel swinging. Light glinted from the tiny blade. It slashed down on his right arm. *Abrupt pain!* Blood darkened the sleeve of his gown.

Orne felt himself caught up in a nightmare. Words leaped to his lips: "Stop that, Lurie! God will punish you!"

Movement behind the child. He looked up.

A toga-clad figure in red turban came striding out of the green wall: a tall man with gleaming eyes, the face of a tortured ascetic—long grey beard parted in the *sufi* manner.

Orne whispered the name: *"Mahmud!"*

A gigantic tri-di of that face dominated the inner mosque of Chargon.

God will punish you!

Orne remembered standing beside his father, staring up at the image in the mosque, bowing to it.

The Mahmud figure strode up behind Lurie, caught her arm as she started another blow. She turned, struggling, but he held her, twisted the arm slowly, methodically. A bone snapped with sickening sharpness. The child screamed and screamed and . . ."

"Don't!" protested Orne.

Mahmud had a low, rumbling voice. He said: "One does not command God's agent to stop His just punishment." He held the child's hair, stooped, caught up the fallen shovel, slashed it across her neck. The screaming stopped. Blood spurted over his gown. He let the now limp figure fall to the floor, dropped the shovel, turned to Orne.

Nightmare! thought Orne. *This has to be a nightmare!*

"You are thinking this is a nightmare," rumbled Mahmud.

And Orne remembered: this creature, too, if it were real,

could think with his reactions and memories. He rejected the thought. "You *are* a nightmare!"

"Your create has done its work," said Mahmud. "It had to be disposed of, you know, because it was embodied by hate, not by love."

Orne felt sickened, guilty, angry. He remembered that this test involved understanding miracles. "This was a miracle?" he demanded.

"What is a miracle?" demanded Mahmud.

Abruptly, an air of suspense enclosed Orne. Prescient fear sucked at his vitals.

"What is a miracle?" repeated Mahmud.

Orne felt his heart hammering. He couldn't seem to focus on the words, stammered: "Are you really an agent of God?"

"Quibbles and labels!" barked Mahmud. "Don't you know about labels? An expediency! There's something *beyond* your labels. Where the zone of the word stops, something else begins."

A tingling sense of madness prickled through Orne. He felt himself balanced on the edge of chaos. "What is a miracle?" he whispered. And he thought back to Emolirdo: *words . . . chaos . . . energy. Psi equals miracle! No. More labels. Energy.*

"Energy from chaos moulded into duration," he said.

"Very close for words," murmured Mahmud. "Is a miracle good or evil?"

"Everybody says miracles are good." Orne took a deep breath. "But they don't have to be either. Good and evil are all tied up in motives."

"Man has motives," said Mahmud.

"Man can be good or evil in his miracles by any definition he wants," said Orne.

Mahmud lifted his head, stared down his nose at Orne. "Yes?"

After a moment of tension, Orne returned the stare. Success in this test had taken on a deep meaning for him. He could feel the inner goading. "Do you want me to say that men create gods to enforce their definitions of good and evil?"

"Do I?"

"So I've said it!"

"Is that all you have to say?"

Orne had to force his attention on to the meanings of words. It was like wading upstream in a swift river. So easy to relax and forget it all. His thoughts showed a tendency to scatter. *Is* what *all I have to say?*

"What is it about men's creations?" demanded Mahmud. "What is it about any creation?"

Orne recalled the nightmare sequence of events in this test. He wondered: *Could this psi machine amplify the energy we call religion? Bakrish said I could bring the dead to life here. Religion's supposed to have a monopoly on that. And the original Mahmud's certainly dead. Been dead for centuries. Provided it isn't hallucination, this whole thing makes a peculiar kind of sense. Even then . . .*

"You know the answer," said Mahmud.

Orne said: "Creations may act independently of their creators. So good and evil don't apply."

"Ah-hah! You have learned this lesson!"

Mahmud stooped, lifted the dead child figure. There was an odd tenderness to his motions. He turned away, marched back into the writhings of the green wall. Silence blanketed the room. The dancing purple lines became almost static, moved in viscous torpor.

Orne felt drained of energy. His arms and legs ached as though he had been using their muscles to the absolute limit.

A bronze clangour echoed behind him, and the green wall returned to its featureless grey. Footsteps slapped against the stone floor. Hands worked at the metallic bowl, lifted it off his head. The straps that held him to the chair fell away. Bakrish came round to stand in front of Orne.

"Did I pass this test?" asked Orne.

"You are alive and still in possession of your soul are you not?"

"How do I know if I still have my soul?"

"One knows by the absence," murmured Bakrish. He glanced down at Orne's wounded arm. "We must get that bandaged. It's night and time for the next step in your ordeal."

"Night?" Orne glanced up at the slitted windows in the dome, saw darkness punctured by stars. He looked around, realized that shadowless exciter light of glow globes had replaced the daylight. "Time goes quickly here."

"For some . . . not for others."

"I feel so tired."

"We'll give you an energy pill when we fix the arm. Come along."

"What's next?"

"You must walk through the shadow of dogma and ceremony, Orne. For it is written that motive is the father of ethics, and caution is the brother of fear . . ." he paused ". . . and fear is the daughter of pain."

There was a nip of chill in the night air. Orne felt thankful now for the thickness of the robe around him. A cooing of birds sounded from the deeper shadows of a park area ahead. Beyond the park arose a hill outlined against the stars, and up the hill marched a snake-track of moving lights.

Bakrish spoke from beside Orne. "The lights are carried by students. Each student has a pole, and on its top a translucent box. The four sides of the boxes each show a different colour: red, blue, yellow and green."

Orne watched the lights. They flickered like weird phosphorescent insects in the dark. "What's the reason for that?"

"They show their piety."

"I mean the four colours?"

"Ah. Red for the blood you dedicate to your god, blue for the truth, yellow for the richness of religious experience, and green for the growth of that experience."

"So they march up the mountain."

"Yes. To show their piety." Bakrish took Orne's arm. "The procession is coming out of the city through a gate in the wall over here. There will be a light for you there. Come along."

They crossed the park, stopped by a narrow open gate. Bakrish took a pole from a rack beside the wall, twisted the handle and light glowed at the top. "Here."

The pole felt slippery smooth in Orne's hand. The light above him was turned to cast a red glow on the people passing through the gate: a student, then a priest, a student, then a priest . . . Their faces carried a uniform gravity.

The end of the procession appeared. "Stay behind that priest," said Bakrish. He urged Orne into the line, fell in behind.

Immediately, prescient fear tugged at Orne's energy. He stumbled, faltered, heard Bakrish grunt: "Keep up! Keep up!"

Orne recovered his balance. His light cast a dull green reflection off the back of the priest ahead. A murmuring, shuffling sounded from the procession. Insects chittered in the tall grass beside their trail. Orne looked up. The bobbing lights wove a meander line up the hill.

The prescient fear grew stronger. Orne felt fragmented. Part of him cowered sickly with the thought that he could fail here. Another part groped out for the chimera of this ordeal. He sensed tremendous elation only a heartbeat away, but this only piled fuel on his fear. It was as though he struggled to awaken from a nightmare within a nightmare, knowing that the pseudo-awakening would only precipitate him into new terror.

The line halted. Orne stumbled to a stop, focused on what was happening around him. Students bunched into a semi-circle. Their lights bounced multicoloured gleams off a stone stupa about twice the height of a man. A bearded priest, his head covered by a red three-cornered hat, his body vague motions under a long black robe, stood in front of the stupa like a dark judge at some mysterious trial.

Orne found a place in the outer ring of students, peered between two of them.

The red-hatted priest bowed, spoke in a resonant bass voice: "You stand before the shrine of purity and the law, the two inseparables of all true belief. Here before you is a key to the great mystery that can lead you to paradise."

Orne felt tension, then the impact of a strong psi field, realized abruptly that this psi field was different. It beat like a metronome with the cadence of the priest's words, rising with the passion of his speech.

". . . the immortal goodness and purity of all the great prophets!" he was saying. "Conceived in purity, born in purity, their thoughts ever bathed in goodness! Untouched by base nature in all their aspects!"

With a shock, Orne realized that this psi field around him arose not from some machine, but from a blending of emotions in the massed students. The emotions he sensed played subtle harmonies on the overriding field. It was as though the priest played these people as a musician might play his instrument.

". . . the eternal truth of this divine dogma!" shouted the priest.

Incense wafted across Orne's nostrils. A hidden voder began to emit low organ notes: a rumbling, sonorous melody. To the right, Orne saw a graveman circling the ring of students and priests waving a censer. Blue smoke hung over the mass of people in ghostly curls. From off in the darkness a bell tinkled seven times.

Orne felt like a man hypnotized, thinking: *Massed emotions act like a psi field! Great God! What* is *a psi field?*

The priest raised both arms, fists clenched. "Eternal paradise to all true believers! Eternal damnation to all unbelievers!" His voice lowered. "You students seeking the eternal truth, fall down to your knees and beg for enlightenment. Pray for the veil to be lifted from your eyes."

There was a shuffling and whisper of robes as the students around Orne sank to their knees. Still Orne stared ahead, his whole being caught up in his discovery. *Massed emotions act like a psi field!*

A muttering sound passed through the students.

What is *a psi field?* Orne asked himself. He felt an answer lurking in a hidden corner of his mind.

Angry glances were directed at Orne from the kneeling students. The muttering grew louder.

Belatedly, Orne became aware of danger. Prescient fear was like a klaxon roaring within him.

Bakrish leaned close, whispered: "There's a trail into the woods off to your right. Better start working towards it."

At the far side of the kneeling crowd a student lifted an arm, pointed at Orne. "What about him? He's a student!"

Someone lost in the mass of people shouted: "Unbeliever!" Others took it up like a mindless chant.

Orne grasped his light standard tightly, began inching his way to the right. Tension in the crowd was like a fuse smoking and sizzling towards a mass of explosives.

The red-hatted priest glared at Orne, dark face contorted in the kaleidoscopic gleams of the students' lights. He thrust out an arm towards Orne. "Death to unbelievers!"

Students began climbing to their feet.

Orne moved faster, stumbling back into the darkness beyond the lights, realized he still carried his own light like a waving beacon. Its coloured reflections picked out a side trail leading off into blackness.

The priest's voice behind him leaped to an insane pitch: "Bring me the head of that blasphemer!"

Orne hurled his light standard like a spear at the suddenly congested group behind him, whirled, fled along the trail.

A ragged, demoniacal yell lifted into the night from the mass of students. A thunder of footsteps pounded after him.

Orne put on more speed. His eyes adjusted to the starlight, and he could just make out the line of the trail curving around the slope to the left. A blotch of deeper blackness loomed ahead.

The woods?

The scrambling mob sound filled the night behind him.

Under Orne's feet, the path became uneven, twisted to the right down a steep slope, turned left. He tripped, almost fell. His robe caught on bushes, and he lost seconds freeing himself, glanced back. Another few seconds and the lights of the mob would reveal him. He came to a split-second decision, plunged off the trail downhill to the right and parallel to the line of trees. Bushes snagged his robe. He fumbled with the belt, shed the robe.

"I hear him!" someone screamed from above.

The mob came to a plunging stop, held silent. Orne's crashing progress dominated the night sounds.

"Down there!"

And they were after him.

"His head!" someone screamed. "Tear his head off him!"

Orne plunged on, feeling cold and exposed in nothing but sandals and the light shorts he had worn beneath the robe. The mob was a crashing avalanche on the hill above him: curses, thumps and tearing sounds, waving lights. Abruptly, Orne stumbled on to another trail, was almost across it before he could turn left. His legs ached. There was a tight band across his chest. He plunged into deeper darkness, glanced up to see trees outlined against the stars. The mob was a confused clamour behind.

Orne stopped, listened to the voices: "Part of you go that way! We'll go this way!"

He drew in gasping breaths, looked around. *Like a hunted animal!* he thought. And he remembered Bakrish's words: "*. . . caution is the brother of fear. . .*" He smiled grimly, slipped off the trail downhill to the right, ducked beneath low limbs, crawled behind a log. Moving softly, silently, he dug dirt from beside the log, smeared it over his face and chest.

Lights came closer along the trail. He heard the angry voices.

Keeping his head down, Orne wriggled deeper into the trees, arose to his knees, slid down a hill. He worked his way to the right down the hill. The mob sounds grew dim, faded.

He crossed another trail, melted through more trees and bushes. His wounded arm ached, and unaccountably this reminded him of the itching sensation he had felt while strapped in the chair . . . *an itching like a healing wound but* before *the wound!* He felt that he had met another clue, but its meaning baffled him.

The trees thinned, bushes grew farther apart. He came out on to the flat park area, a lawn underfoot. Beyond the park he saw the wall, and above that street lights and glowing windows.

Bakrish said the Halmyrach Abbod is in this city, thought Orne. *Why bother with the lower echelons? I'm a field agent of the I–A. It's time I got down to work.* And in the back of his mind another thought niggled: *Did I pass that last test?* Angrily, he pushed the thought aside, crouched as footsteps sounded on a path to his left.

Through the thin starlight filtered by scattered trees he saw a priest in white walking along the path. Orne flattened himself against a tree, waited. Fragrance of night-blooming flowers crossed his nostrils. Birds whirring and rustling sounded from the branches overhead. The footsteps came closer.

Orne waited for the priest to pass, slipped out behind him.

Presently, Orne strode towards the wall and the street lights. The priest's robe hung a little long. He tucked a fold under the belt, smiled. In the dark bushes at the edge of the park lay an unconscious figure bound and gagged with strips torn from his own underclothing.

Now, we see what makes this place tick, thought Orne. He paused while still in the shadows of the park, scrubbed at the dirt on his face and chest with an undercorner of the robe, then continued on his way calmly—a priest out on normal business.

No movement showed beyond the low wall. Orne walked along it, entered by a gate, crossed to an alley. A sour smell of cooking tainted the narrow way. The slapping of his sandalled feet made a double echo off the stone walls. Ahead, a standard light showed the crossing of another narrow alley.

Orne stopped as thin shadows projected across the intersection. Two priests strode into view. Orne hurried ahead, recalled a religious greeting from his own childhood training on Chargon. "Shari'a, gentle sirs," he said. "God grant you peace."

The pair stopped with their faces in shadows half turned his direction. The near one spoke: "May you follow the highway of divine command and guidance." The other said: "May we be of service?"

"I am from another sector and have been summoned to the Halmyrach Abbod," said Orne. "I seem to have lost my way." He waited, alert to every movement from the pair.

"These alleys are like a maze," said the nearest priest. "But you are near." He turned, and the street light revealed a pinched-in face, narrow eyes. "Take the next turning to your right. Follow that way to the third turning left. That street ends at the court of the Abbod."

"I am grateful," murmured Orne.

"A service to one of God's creatures is a service to God," said the priest. "May you find wisdom." The pair bowed, passed around Orne, went on their way.

Orne smiled into the darkness, thinking: *Old I–A maxim—Go straight to the top.*

The street of the Abbod proved to be even narrower than the others. Orne could have stretched out his arms to touch both walls. At the end of the alley a door glowed dimly grey in reflected starlight. The door proved to be locked.

A locked door? he thought. *Can all be sweetness and purity here?* He stepped back, peered up at the wall. Dark irregularities there suggested spikes or a similar barrier. His thought was cynically amused: *Such civilized appointments on this peaceful planet!*

A glance back up the alley showed it still empty. He shed the priestly robe, swung a hemmed corner up on to the wall, pulled. The robe slipped back slightly, caught. There was a small tearing sound as he tested it, but the robe held. He tried his weight on it. The fabric stretched, but remained firmly caught.

Scrabbling sounds marked his passage up the wall. He avoided sharp spikes on the top, crouched there. One window in the building opposite him glowed with a dim rose colour behind loose draperies. He glanced down, saw a starlit courtyard, tall pots in rows topped with flowering bushes. Another glance at the window, and he felt the abrupt stab of prescient fear. *Danger there!* An air of tension hung over the courtyard.

Orne freed the robe from the spike, dropped into the courtyard, crouched in shadows while he slipped back into the priest's garment. One deep breath, and he began working his way around the courtyard to the left, hugging the shadows. Vines dropped from a balcony below the lighted window. He tested one, found it too fragile, moved farther along the wall. A draught touched his left cheek. Darker blackness there—an open door.

Prescient fear tingled along his nerves. Angrily, he put down the fear, slipped through the door into the hall.

Light glared in the hall!

Orne froze, then suppressed laughter as he saw the beam switch beside the door. He stepped back: darkness. Forward: light.

Stairs climbed curving to the left at the end of the hall. Orne moved quietly along the hall, paused at the foot of the stairs and looked up at a heavy wooden door with golden initials on it in bas relief: "H.A."

Halmyrach Abbod! Right to the top!

He slipped up the stairs, cautiously gripped the door handle, turned it with the gentlest of pressure. The lock clicked. He threw the door open, lunged through, slammed the door behind him.

"Ah, Mr Orne. Very resourceful of you." It was a faintly tenor masculine voice with just an edge of quaver to it.

Orne slewed around, saw a wide-hooded bed. Remote in

the bed like a dark-skinned doll sat a man in a nightshirt. He was propped up by a mound of pillows. The face looked familiar. It was narrow, smooth-skinned with a nose that hung like a precipice over a wide mouth. His head was polished dark baldness.

The wide mouth moved, and the faintly quavering tenor voice said: "I am the Halmyrach Abbod. You wished to see me?"

An aura of oldness hung over the man in the bed like an ancient odour of parchment.

Orne took two steps towards the bed, his prescient fear clamouring. He paused, recalling the resemblance. "You look like Emolirdo."

"My younger brother, Mr Orne. Do be seated." He gestured towards a chair beside the bed. "Forgive me for receiving you this way, but I find myself jealous of my rest in these later years."

Orne moved to the chair. Something about this skinny ancient spoke of deadliness beyond anything Orne had ever before encountered. He glanced around the room, saw dark hangings on the walls covered with weird shapes: curves and squares, pyramids, swastikas and a repetitive symbol like an anchor—a vertical line with an arc at its base. The floor was black and white tile of gigantic pentagonal pieces, each at least two metres across. Furniture of polished woods was crowded into the corners: a desk, a low table, chairs, a tape rack and a stand in the shape of a spiral staircase.

"Have you already summoned your guards?" asked Orne.

"I have no need of them, Mr Orne. Please sit down." Again the skeletal arm gestured towards the chair.

Orne looked at the chair. It had no arms to conceal secret bindings.

"The chair is just a chair," said the Abbod.

Orne sat down like a man plunging into cold water, tensed.

The Abbod smiled. "You see?"

Orne wet his lips with his tongue. Something was wrong

here. This was not working out at all as he had imagined. "I came here to find out some things," he said.

"Good. We shall share information."

"Why're you people out to get the I–A?"

"First things first, Mr Orne. Have you deciphered the intent of your ordeal?" The Abbod's large eyes, brown and glossy, stared at Orne. "Do you know why you co-operated with us?"

"What else could I do?"

"Many things, as you have demonstrated just this night."

"All right, I was curious."

"About what?"

Orne lowered his eyes, felt something quicken within himself.

"Be honest with yourself, Mr Orne."

"I . . . I suspected you were teaching me things about myself that . . . that I didn't already know."

"Superb!" The Abbod smiled. "But you were a product of the Marakian civilization. All aberrative tendencies had been removed at an early age by microsurgical *atenture*. How, then, could there be left anything about yourself that you did not know?"

"There just *was*. I found out I could be afraid without knowing why. I . . ."

"Had you ever heard of the thaumaturgic psychiatrists of the ancient Christian era?"

"What era was that?"

"Long ago. So long ago that there are left only small, tantalizing fragments to tell us of those days. The Christeros religion derives from that period."

"What about it?"

"You have not heard of these ancient practices?"

"I know there were mental sciences before the microsurgical techniques were developed. Is that what you mean?"

"In a way." The Abbod fell silent, waiting.

Orne swallowed. This was not going the way it should

have gone. He felt on the defensive, and all he faced was one skinny old man in a ridiculous nightshirt. Anger swelled in Orne. "I came here to find out if you people were fomenting war!"

"And what if we were? What then? Were you prepared to be the surgeon, to cut out the infection and leave society in its former health?"

Orne's anger receded.

"Do you not see the parallel, Mr Orne?" The Abbod frowned. "The best of a supreme mechanistic science worked you over and declared you sane, balanced, clear. Yet there remained something more that they had not touched."

"Then there's something the I–A isn't . . . touching?"

"But of course."

"What?"

"Most of every iceberg is beneath the surface of the sea," said the Abbod.

A tiny wave of Orne's anger surged back. "Now what's *that* supposed to mean?"

"Then let us approach it this way," said the Abbod. "The Guru called Pasawan, who led the Ramakrishnanas into the Great Unifying we know as the Ecumenical Truce, was a follower of the Hynd doctrine. This has always taught the divinity of the soul, the unity of all existence, the oneness of the Godhead and the harmony of all religions."

Orne stiffened. "You're not going to get anywhere trying to force a lot of religious pap down my throat!"

"One does not successfully force religion on to anyone," murmured the Abbod. "If it pleases you to do so, you may consider this in the nature of a history lesson."

Orne sank back in the chair. "So get on with it."

"Thanks to Pasawan, we believe we have developed here a science of religion. The discovery of psi powers and an interpretation of their significance tends to confirm our postulates."

"Which are?"

"That mankind, acting somewhat as a great psi machine, does create a force, an energy system. We may refer to this system as religion, and invest it with an independent focus of action which we will call God. But remember that a god without discipline faces the same fate as the merest human under the same circumstances. It is unfortunate that mankind has always been so attracted by visions of absolutes—even in his gods."

Orne recalled his experience that night when he had felt a psi field surging out of the emotions in the massed students. He rubbed his chin.

"Let us consider this idea of absolutes," said the Abbod. "Let us postulate a finite system in which a given *being* may exhaust all avenues of knowledge—know everything, as it were."

In an intuitive leap, Orne saw the image being painted by the Abbod's words. He blurted: "It'd be worse than death!"

"Unutterable, deadly boredom would face such a being. Its future would be endless repetition, replaying all of its old tapes. A boredom worse than extinction."

"But boredom is a kind of stasis," said Orne. "Stasis would lead to chaos."

"And what do we have?" asked the Abbod. "We have chaos: an infinite system where *any*thing can happen—a place of constant change. And let us recognize one of the inevitable properties of this infinite system. If *any*thing can happen, then our hypothetical *being* could be extinguished. Quite a price to pay to escape boredom, eh?"

"All right. I'll go along with your game and your hypothetical *being*. Couldn't it find some kind of . . . well, insurance?"

"Such as scattering its eggs in an infinite number of baskets, eh?"

"Life's done just that, hasn't it? It's scattered all over the universe in billions of forms."

"Yet *any*thing can happen," murmured the Abbod. "So we have two choices: infinite boredom or infinite chance."

"So what?"

"Do you wish me to continue with the history lesson?"

"Go ahead."

"Now, behind or beneath or projecting into this scattered *Life*, let us postulate a kind of consciousness that . . ." He raised a hand as Orne's face darkened. "Hear me out, Mr Orne. "This *other* consciousness has been suspected for countless centuries. It has been called such things as 'collective unconscious', 'the paramatman', 'urgrund', 'sanatana dharma', 'super mind', 'ober palliat' . . . It has been called many things."

"None of which makes it any more real!" snapped Orne. "Let's not mistake *clear* reasoning for *correct* reasoning. The fact that a name exists for something doesn't mean that thing exists."

"You are then an empiricist," said the Abbod. "Good. Did you ever hear the legend of Doubting Thomas?"

"No."

"No matter," said the Abbod. "He was always one of my favourite characters. He refused to take crucial facts on faith."

"Sounds like a wise man."

The Abbod smiled. "A moment ago I said that mankind generates a power we may call religion, and within that religion a focus of independent action you may refer to as God."

"Are you sure it isn't the other way around?"

"That's of no importance at the moment, Mr Orne. Let us go on to a corollary of the original postulate, which is that mankind also generates prophets in the same way—men who point out the paths that lead to degeneracy and failure. And here we come to a function of our order as I see it. We find these prophets and educate them."

"You educate men like Mahmud?"

"Mahmud escaped us."

Orne suddenly sat up straight. "Are you implying that *I'm* a prophet?"

"But of course you are. You're a man with extraordinary powers. Psi instruments have only sharpened and brought to focus what was already there, latent within you."

Orne slapped a hand on to his right knee. "If this isn't the wildest train of . . ."

"I'm serious, Mr Orne. In the past, prophets have tended to preach without restriction—uninhibited and really un-disciplined. The results were always the same: temporary order that climbed towards greater and greater power, then the inevitable degeneration. We, on the other hand, have another method. We seek the slow, self-disciplined ac-cumulation of data that will extend our science of religion. The broad course ahead of us is already becoming . . ."

"Do you mean to tell me that you people presume to educate prophets?"

An inner light glittered in the Abbod's glossy eyes. "Mr Orne, have you any idea how many innocents have been tortured to death in the name of religion during the course of Man's bloody history?"

Orne shrugged. "There's no way of knowing how many."

"Countless?"

"Certainly."

"That is one of the things which always happen when religions run wild, Mr Orne. War and bloodshed of countless sorts develop from undisciplined religion."

"And you think I'm a prophet?"

"We *know* you are. It is uncertain whether you could start a new religion, but you *are* a prophet. We had you out on that mountainside tonight for just one purpose. Your fellow students did not turn out to be prophets. They will never rise above the oblate brotherhood. We know their character, however, and we know your character. Put the two together, and you should have learned a lesson."

"Sure! That I could get my head torn off by a mob!"

"That would have meant you failed the test," said the Abbod. "Now, please be calm and tell me the basic significance of your experience out there."

"Wait a minute," said Orne. "How'd *you* know what happened out there?"

"I knew within seconds when you ran away from the mob," said the Abbod. "I was waiting for the report. We suspected you would come here."

"Of course. And you just sat here and waited for me."

"Of course. Now answer the question: What's the basic significance of your experience?"

Orne turned his head, looked out of the corners of his eyes at the Abbod. "That there's a great amount of explosive energy in religion. That's what I learned."

"You already knew this, naturally."

"Yes. You just made the fact important to me."

"Mr Orne, I will tell you about just one of the many prophets we have on Amel. His talents are extreme. He can cause a glowing aura to appear around his body. He can levitate. What we understand as space does not exist for him. Seemingly, he can step from planet to planet as easily as a normal person would cross the . . ."

"Is this that fellow who was on Wessen? The one the feature scribes went nuts over when . . ."

"I see you've heard of him. We got to him barely in time, Mr Orne. I ask you now: What would happen if he were to appear to a crowd, say, on Marak, that enlightened centre of our government, and display there his full powers?"

Orne frowned.

"Is it likely they would put a religious interpretation on his activities?" demanded the Abbod.

"Well . . . probably."

"Most certainly! And what if he did not fully understand his own talents? Picture it. He knows the true from the false by some inner sense—call it instinct. Around him he sees much that is false. What's he likely to do?"

"All right!" barked Orne. "He'd probably start a new religion! You've made your point."

"A *wild* religion," corrected the Abbod. He glared at Orne, pointed to Orne's left. "Look there!"

Orne turned, saw a dancing sword of flame about two metres away. Its point was aimed at his head. He shivered, felt perspiration drench his body. Prescient fear screamed within him.

"The first lone man to tap that source of energy was burned alive as a sorcerer by his fellow humans," said the Abbod. "The ancients thought that flame was alive. They gave it religious significance, called it a *salamander*. They thought of it as a demon. And when you don't know how to control it, the thing does act like a wild demon with a life and will of its own. It's raw energy, Mr Orne. *I* direct it through a psi focus. You act so superior. You think of yourself as a servant of a great organization that prevents war. Yet I—one man alone—could utterly annihilate any military force you could bring against me . . . and I would use nothing but this ancient discovery!"

The old man sank back against his pillows, closed his eyes. Presently, he opened his eyes, said: "Sometimes I forget my years, but they never forget me."

Orne drew in a ragged breath. The deadliness that he had suspected in this skeletal human had taken on form and dimension: deadliness magnified to new dimensions.

"When Emolirdo informed us of you, we had to bring you here, test you, see for ourselves," murmured the Abbod. "So many do not test out. In your case, though, the tests proved Emolirdo correct. You . . . ."

"I did things Emolirdo taught me how to do, and *with* equipment he had put in my body!"

"Your *equipment* has been nullified by a dampening projection since your interview with Bakrish at your arrival," said the Abbod.

Orne opened his mouth to protest, closed it. He recalled his sensation of strangeness during that first interview. *Nullified?* Yet he still sensed danger all around.

"What Emolirdo did was to force you to accept the things you already could do," said the Abbod. "Your first lesson: faith in yourself." He looked grimly amused. "But it is plain that you still cherish doubts."

"You're damn' right I do! I think this whole hocus pocus was designed to confuse me, put me off the track!"

"You doubt the existence of a superior consciousness that manifests itself in gods and prophets and even sometimes in our machines," said the Abbod.

"I think you may have stumbled on to something with your psi powers, but you've mucked it up with your mystical hogwash! There's a scientific explanation for these things that'd appear if you blew away all this fog."

"The empiricist demands his demonstration," murmured the Abbod. "Very well. Let us introduce you to the graduate school, Mr Orne. Thus far, you've been playing with toys. Let's see how you react when we threaten the basic fibre of your being!"

Orne pushed himself to his feet, reached behind for the back of the chair. He glanced left at the dancing point of flame, saw it sweep around in front of his eyes. Burning, prickling sensations crawled along his skin. The flame grew to a ball almost a metre in diameter, pressed forwards. Orne stumbled backwards, knocked over the chair. Heat blasted his face.

"How now?" cried the Abbod.

He's trying to panic me, thought Orne. *This could be an illusion.* He darted to the left, and the flame shot ahead of him, cutting him off, pressed even closer.

Orne retreated. His face burned where the flame seared against it.

"Is this illusion, Mr Orne?" called the Abbod.

Doggedly, Orne shook his head. His eyes smarted. The flaming ball pressed him backwards. He shook perspiration from his head, glanced down at the floor. *Pentagonal tiles. Giant pentagonal tiles at least two metres across.* He stepped to the centre of a white tile, immediately felt the heat diminish.

"Psi must be faced with psi," called the Abbod.

Orne nodded, wet his lips with his tongue, swallowed. He tried to focus on the inner awareness as Emolirdo had taught him. Nothing. He closed his eyes, concentrated, felt something give.

Somewhere, there was a great howling of not-sound. He was being pulled inwards, distorted. Twisted in a vortex that sucked him down . . . down . . . down . . . down . . .

The thought of ticking seconds blazed within him.

TIME!

No sensation except a dim touch of the pentagram as though it pressed against his body at every point: a pentagram, a box, a cage. And the ticking seconds. His mind boiled with the thought of *TIME!*

Time and tension, he thought. And his mind juggled symbols like blocks of energy, manipulated energy like discrete signals. There was a problem. *Tension! Tension = energy source. Energy + opposition = growth of energy. To strengthen a thing, oppose it. Growth of energy + opposition = opposites blending into a new identity.*

"You become like the worst in what you oppose," he thought. It was a quotation. He had heard it somewhere. *Priest slips into evil. The great degenerates into the small.*

And he remembered his wounded arm, the itching before the wound.

TIME!

Beyond the pentagram he sensed a place where chaotic energy flowed. A great blank not-darkness filled with not-light and a ceaseless flowing. And he felt himself as on a mountaintop—as though he *were* the mountaintop. Pressing upwards but still connected to a living earth below. Somewhere he felt the touch of the pentagram: a shape that could be remembered and located.

A voice came from below the mountain: "Mr Orne?"

He felt the pentagram press more tightly.

"Mr Orne?"

The Abbod's voice.

Orne felt himself flowing back, compressed, twisted. The shape of his body became a new distortion to his senses. He wanted to resist.

"Don't fight it, Mr Orne."

Pressure against side and arms: the floor. He opened his

eyes, found that he was stretched out on the tiles, his head at one corner of the white pentagram, his feet at the opposite corner. The Abbod stood over him in a belted white robe: a dark, monkey-like creature with overlarge, staring eyes.

"What did you see? Mr Orne?"

Orne drew in a deep, gasping breath. He felt dizzy, weak. "Nothing," he gasped.

"Oh, yes. You *saw* with every sense you possess. One does not walk without seeing the path."

Walk? Path? Orne remembered the sense of flowing chaos. He pulled his arms back, pushed himself up. The floor felt cold against his palms. The wound in his arm itched. He shook his head. "What do you *want* from me?"

The Abbod's gaze bored into him. "*You* tell me."

Orne swallowed in a dry throat. "I saw chaos."

The Abbod leaned forward. "And *where* is this chaos?"

Orne looked down at his feet extended along the floor, glanced around the room, back to the Abbod. "Here. It was this world, this universe, this . . ."

"Why could you see it as chaos?"

Orne shook his head. *Why? I was threatened. I . . . TIME!* He looked up. "It has something to do with time."

"Mr Orne, have you ever seen a jungle?"

"Yes."

"The plant life, its growth is not immediately apparent to your senses, is it?"

"Not . . . immediately. But over a period of days, of course, you . . ." He broke off.

"Precisely!" barked the Abbod. "If you could, as it were, speed up the jungle, it would become a place of writhing contention. Vines would shoot up like snakes to clutch and strangle the trees. Plants would leap upwards, blast forth with pods, hurl out their seeds. You would see a great strangling battle for sunlight."

"Time," said Orne. And he recalled Emolirdo's analogy: the three-dimensional shadow cast into the two-dimensional world. "How does the person in the two-dimensional world interpret the shadow of a three-dimensional object?" he murmured.

The Abbod smiled. "Emolirdo so enjoys that analogy."

"The two-dimensional being can interpolate," said Orne. "He can stretch his imagination to create . . . *things* that reach into the other dimension."

"So?"

Orne felt the tension. Nerves trembled along his arms. "Psi machines!" he blurted. "They manipulate time!"

"Psi phenomena are time phenomena," said the Abbod.

It was like veils falling away from Orne's senses. He remembered his wounded arm, the itching he had felt before the arm was wounded in that exact place. He recalled a small psi instrument that Emolirdo had displayed: loops, condensers, electronic tubes, all focusing on a thin square of plastic. Rubbed one way, the plastic felt tacky. Rubbed the other way, the plastic felt as slick as glass, greased.

In a half-musing way, he said: "There was a thin layer of time flow along the plastic. One direction, my hand moved with the flow; the other direction, my hand opposed the flow."

"Eh?" The Abbod looked puzzled.

"I was remembering something," said Orne.

"Oh." The Abbod turned, shuffled back to his bed, sat on the edge. His robe opened, revealing thin shanks under his nightshirt. He looked incredibly old and tired.

Orne felt a pang of sympathy for the old man. The sense of dread that had surrounded this place was gone. In its place he felt an awakening akin to awe.

"Life projects matter through the dimension of time," said the Abbod.

"A kind of time machine?"

The Abbod nodded. "Yes. Our awareness is split. It exists within these three dimensions and outside of them. We have known this for centuries. Thoughts can blaze through a lifetime in the merest fraction of a second. Threaten the human life, and you can force his awareness to retreat into no-time. You can weigh countless alternatives, select the course of action that has the greatest survival potential. All of this you can do while time in this dimension stands still."

Orne took a deep breath. He knew this was true. He recalled that final terrible instant in the Heleb uprising. There he had sat at the controls of his escape ship while around him great weapons swung about to bear on the vessel's flimsy walls. There seemed no way to avoid the blasting energies that were sure to come. And he remembered the myriad alternatives that had flitted through his mind while outside the terrible weapons seemed to hang frozen. And he *had* escaped. The one sure way had been seen.

The Abbod pushed himself back into the bed, pulled covers over his legs. "I am a very old man." He looked sideways at Orne. "But it still pleasures me to see a person make the *old* discovery."

Orne took a step forward. "Old?"

"Ancient. Thousands of years before the first man ventured into space from the original home world, a scattered few were discovering this way of looking at the universe. They called it *Mayá*. The tongue was Sanskrit. Our view of the matter is a little more . . . sophisticated. But there's no essential difference. The ancients said: '*Abandon forms; direct yourself towards temporal reality.*' You know, Mr Orne, it's amazing. Man has such an . . . *appetite* to encompass . . . *everything*."

Like a sleep walker, Orne moved forward, righted the chair beside the bed, sank into it. Extensions of his awakening captured his attention. "*The prophet who calls forth the dead,*" he said. "*He returns the matter of the body to a time when it was alive.* That flame you threatened me with. You bring it out of a time when the matter around us was gaseous incandescence. The man from Wessen who walks from planet to planet like you would cross a stream on stepping stones." Orne held up his hands. "Of course. Without time to stretch across it, there can be no space. To him, *time is a specific location!*"

"Think of the universe as an expanding balloon," said the

Abbod. "A balloon of weird shape and unexplored convolutions. Suppose you have a transparent grid, three-dimensional. Like graph paper. You look through it at the universe. It is a matrix against which you can plot out the shapes and motions of the universe."

"Education," said Orne.

The Abbod spoke like a teacher praising a pupil. "Very good!" He smiled. "This grid, this matrix is trained into human beings. They project it on to the universe. With this matrix they break nature into bits. Usable bits. But, somehow, they too often get the idea that nature . . . the universe *is* the bits. The matrix is so very useful, permitting us to communicate our ideas, for example. But it is so near-sighted. It's like an old man reading script with his nose pressed almost to the page. He sees one thing at a time. But our universe is *not* one thing at a time. It's an enormous complex. Still we concentrate on the bits." He shook his head. "Do you know how we see the bits, Mr Orne?"

Orne snapped out of a half-reverie in which the Abbod's words had been like gross areas of understanding that flowed into his awareness. "We see them by contrast. Each bit moves differently, has a different colour, or . . ."

"Very good! We see them by contrast. To see a bit we must see also its background. Bit and background are inseparable. Without one you cannot discern the other. Without evil you cannot determine good. Without war, you cannot determine peace. Without . . ."

"Wait a minute!" Orne jerked to attention. "Is that why you're out to ruin the I–A?"

"Mr Orne, a compulsive peace is not peace. To compel peace, you must use warlike methods. It is nonsense to think that you can get rid of one of a pair and possess only the other. You are doing this by force! You create a vacuum into which chaos will flow."

Orne shook his head. He felt trapped in a maze, caught by the idea that something *had* to be wrong with the Abbod's words.

"It is like a drug habit," said the Abbod. "If you enforce peace, it will take greater and greater amounts of peace to satisfy you. And you will use more and more violence to obtain it. The cycle will end in cataclysm. Think rather of how light reaches your eyes. When you are reading you do not seek out, striving for the light. In the same way, peace comes to your senses. Pleasure comes to you. Good comes to you. As the light reaches your eyes. These are functions of your nerves. You cannot make an effort with your nerves. You *can* make an effort with your muscles. That is the way it is with our universe. Our matrix must be a direct function of reality, of actual matter. In this, it is like our nerves. If we distort the matrix, we do not change reality, but only our way of seeing it. If we destroy one half of a pair, the remaining half overwhelms us. Take away the predator, and the creature preyed upon undergoes a population explosion. All of these things fit the basic law."

"And the I–A has broken that law?"

"It has." The Abbod frowned. "You see, peace is an internal matter. It's a *self*-discipline. It *must* come from within. If you set up an outside power to *enforce* peace, that outside power grows stronger and stronger. It must. Inevitably, it degenerates. Comes the cataclysm."

"You people on Amel look on yourselves as a kind of super I–A, don't you?"

"In a sense," the Abbod agreed. "But we want to go to the root. We wish to plant the seed of self-discipline wherever it will take root. And to do this, we prepare certain ground for cultivation."

"Ground?"

"Worlds. Societies." The Abbod stared at Orne. "And we desperately need farmers, Mr Orne."

"Meaning me?"

"Would you care to enlist?"

Orne cleared his throat, broke his attention away from the Abbod's intent gaze. He felt that he was being stampeded.

The Abbod's voice intruded. "This is a chaotic universe,

Mr Orne. Things are changing. Things *will* change. There is an instinct in human beings that realizes this. Our instinct foments a feeling of insecurity. We seek something unchanging. Beliefs are temporary because the bits we believe *about* are in motion. They change. And periodically, we go through the cataclysm. We tear down the things that refuse to work. They don't do what we expect them to do, and we become children, smashing the toys that refuse to obey. In such times, the teachers of self-discipline are much needed."

"You say we're approaching some great smashing up, some cataclysm?"

"We are always approaching it. Always ahead of us is the great burning from which the Phoenix arises. Only one thing endures: Faith. The object changes, but faith endures. It's the absolute we yearn after in a changing universe."

Orne felt overwhelmed by a sense of outrage. "Faith? That's nonsense! There's no logic, no scientific . . ."

"Trust your senses!" barked the Abbod. "Do not try to distort the matrix to fit what you *want* to believe! You have experienced another dimension. Many have done this without realizing it. *You* realize it."

"But . . . faith? In what?"

"In our appetite. Faith that we will encompass this other dimension and find there a new area of mystery to beckon our senses. Faith that there is something enduring in all this chaos . . . and if not, that we can create a thing that will endure. *That* faith, Mr Orne.'

Orne lowered his eyes. "I'm sorry. I . . . didn't understand."

The Abbod's voice lowered almost to a whisper. "Of course you didn't. You had not heard our simple definition of a religion. A religion is the faith that something will endure beyond the apparent chaos surrounding us. The central concepts are Faith and Endurance."

Orne turned the thought over in his mind.

"Our faith here is in the linear endurance of humankind," said the Abbod. "On Amel we call it the Great Continuity. It is our faith that there will always be a descendant of humankind—evolved, changed, unrecognizable to today's humans, no matter what, but still our descendant."

Cynicism, his most dependable defence, took over Orne's thinking. "Very high sounding," he said. "And if that's what you're really doing here, quite attractive. But how can I be certain what you're doing? You use lots of words. Some even make sense."

"But all it takes is one weak link, eh?"

Orne shrugged.

"That's why we seek out only the strong, the prophets," said the Abbod. "That is why the testing and the education. If we tame the wild religions and harness their energies to our purpose, that makes sense, doesn't it?"

"Certainly."

"Then we will give you this, Mr Orne: You may go anywhere on Amel, ask any questions, look at any records, request any co-operation that does not oppose our purpose. Satisfy yourself. And even then, you do not have to decide to stay with us. You may return to any of the outer worlds, to Marak, to Chargon, wherever you wish to go. We insist only that you subject your talents to our instructions, that you permit us to show you how they may be tamed."

Orne wet his lips with his tongue. A tentative probe at the Abbod's emotions revealed candour and faint amusement. The amusement annoyed Orne. He had the feeling that this was an old story to the Abbod, that the reactions of one Lewis Orne could be classified as type such and so. A kind of pique made him say: "Aren't you afraid I might . . . well, double-cross you once I was off Amel?"

"We have faith in *you*, Mr Orne. Your ordeal has given us grounds for that, at least."

Orne chuckled. "The least I can do is return the favour, eh?"

"After you've pried and tested us to your satisfaction, yes. You said it yourself, you know: Faith is the uncensored will. Doubt is a censor we'd rather you didn't have."

Orne nodded, and a new thought hit him. "Do you have enough faith in me to let me return to Marak and make over the I–A along lines you'd approve?"

The Abbod shook his head. "Faith in you, we have that. But your I–A has gone too far along the road to power. You understand, my son, that a bureau is like an individual. It will fight for survival. It will seek power. Your I–A has a personality made up of all its parts. Some such as yourself we would trust. Others . . . I'm afraid not. No. Before we permit you to leave here, the I–A will be dead, and other bureaus will be feeding on the remains."

Orne stared at the ancient face. Presently, he said: "I guess I failed them."

"Perhaps not. Your original purpose is still intact. Peace as a self-discipline can be more gratifying than any other kind. It grows more slowly, to be sure, but it's confident growth that counts."

Orne still tasted a certain bitterness. "You seem pretty confident that I'll join you."

"You've already passed that decision," murmured the Abbod. "When you asked to return and make over the I–A."

This time Orne's chuckle was aimed at himself. "Know me pretty well, don't you."

"We know your purpose, your religion, as it were. You share our faith in humankind. When we learned that, we knew you were already one of us." The Abbod smiled, and the old face seemed to light up. "There's much ground to prepare, and we have need of many farmers."

"Yeah, I'm a hayseed, all right," said Orne.

"After you have pried into Amel to your heart's content, come back and talk to me. I know there's a certain young lady awaiting you on Marak. Perhaps we could discuss your returning to another bureau—Rediscovery and Re-education."

"R & R! Those bumbleheads! They're the . . ."

"You have an interesting conditioned reaction there," said the Abbod. "For now I will only remind you that any bureau is the sum of its parts."

*   *   *

In his office on Marak, Tyler Gemine, director of Rediscovery & Re-education, faced Orne across an immense blackwood desk. Behind Gemine a wide window looked out on the packed office buildings of Marak's central government quarter. The director was a rounded outline against the window, a fat and genial surface with smiling mouth and hard eyes. Frown wrinkles creased his forehead.

The office fitted Gemine. On the surface it seemed built for comfort: soft chairs, thick carpet, unobtrusive lighting. But three walls held file cases geared to a remote search control at the desk. Six auto-secretaries flanked the desk.

Sitting opposite the director, Orne still wore his aqua toga from Amel. R & R security police had rushed him here from the spaceport, giving him no time to change.

"All of this haste must appear unseemly to you, Mr Orne," said Gemine. "Separating you from your fiancée at the spaceport like that. Rude of us." The hard eyes bored into Orne.

Orne hid his amusement under a mask of concern. "I know you must have good reasons, sir."

Gemine leaned back. "Indeed we do." He pulled a stack of papers towards him on the desk, squared them. "Before the I–A took you away from us, Mr Orne, you were an agent of the R & R."

"Yes, sir. They drafted me."

"That unfortunate business on Hamal!"

"There was nothing I could do, sir."

"No blame attaches to you, Mr Orne. But you understand that we do have some curiosity about you now that we have superseded the I–A."

"You want to know where my loyalties are?"

"Precisely."

"The R & R's purpose is still my purpose, sir."

"Good! Good!" Gemine patted the stack of papers in front of him. "Ahhh, this mission to Amel. What about that?"

"Why was I sent?"

Gemine's stare was cold and measuring. "Yes."

"It was very simple. The I–A executive staff heard about the move to do away with their department. They had reason to believe the priests were a prime factor in the move. I was sent to Amel to see if they could be circumvented."

"And you failed." It was a flat statement.

"Sir, I beg to remind you that I once volunteered for the R & R. I was one of your agents before the I–A took me away from you." He managed a tight smile. "And it didn't take a giant brain to realize that you would take over the I–A's functions once they were out of the way."

Gemine's eyes clouded with thought. He cleared his throat. "What about this psi thing? In the final audit of I–A we came across this odd department. Unfortunately . . ." Gemine studied a paper in front of him. " . . . the director, one Ag Emolirdo, has disappeared. There were records, though, showing that you were trained by him before your recent . . . ah, mission."

So Agony took it on the lam, thought Orne. *Gone home to report, no doubt.* He said: "It was a questionable field. Oriented along ESP lines." (And he thought: *That'll fit this little hack's executive logic!*) "They were looking for rules to explain certain non-chance phenomena," he went on. "Their results were debatable."

Gemine restacked the papers in front of him. "As I suspected. Well . . . we can go into it in more detail later. I confess it sounded extremely far-fetched in outline. Typical of I–A wastefulness." He leaned back, steepled his hands in front of him. "No, Mr Orne, as you know, we are taking over the key functions of the I–A. But we're running into stupid resistance. That's where I've hoped you could come in."

"My record with R & R is clear, sir."

Gemine swivelled his chair, looked out of the window at Marak's executive warren. "You know both the R & R and the I–A, Mr Orne. It's in my mind to attach you to my office—as a special executive assistant. Your duties would be to facilitate absorption of the I–A." He turned back to look at Orne. "What would you say to that?"

Orne hesitated just the right length of time. "I'd . . . I'd consider that an honour, sir."

"Excellent!" Gemine bent forward. "You'll want to get situated first, of course." His manner became more confidential. "You'll be getting married, I understand. Take what time you need. Say, a month."

"That's very kind of you, sir."

"Not at all. I want you to be happy with us." He wet his lips with his tongue. "Miss Bullone may not have had the time to tell you . . . about her father, that is. He is no longer our high commissioner. Lost out in the recent shake-up. A pity after so many years of excellent service."

"Has he stayed on in the Assembly?"

"Oh, yes. He's still an important member. Minority leader." Gemine stared at Orne. "We'd like to have you act—unofficially, you understand—as a sort of liaison with Mr Bullone."

"I'm sure something could be worked out, sir."

Gemine smiled, relaxed. He nodded.

Orne said: "What about my staff, sir?"

"Staff?"

"I'll need assistants of my own if I'm to do this job correctly."

Sudden tension filled the room. "Anyone special in mind?"

Gently, thought Orne. *This is the delicate part.* He said: "All the time I was in the I–A, I was directly under one man. When he said frog, I jumped. Wherever he pointed, that's where I went."

"Ahhh . . . Mr Umbo Stetson."

"I see you know him."

"Know him? He's a major source of resistance!"

"That'd make it even more pleasant," said Orne.

Gemine chortled. He radiated gleeful sadism. "Take him! Any authority you need to whip him into line, it's yours!"

Orne matched Gemine's smile. "This is going to be even more fun than I thought."

Gemine arose. "I'll have an office fitted for you next to mine, Lewis. Want everything cosy and neat." He nodded. "I think this is going to work out very well. Indeed I do."

Orne stood up. "I hope I'll live up to all your expectations, sir."

"You already are, my boy! You know what's expected of you, and you know how to deliver." He gave Orne a knowing smile. "And I won't soon forget your *failure* on Amel." He chortled. "Eh?"

From the secret report: Lewis Orne to the Halmyrach Abbod:

Gemine was every bit as easy as you said he would be. He has already given me Stetson, and through Stetson I'll bring in the others. This is fallow ground, indeed. Needs the ministrations of a trained farmer.

It was fascinating to talk to Gemine. There was the pattern just as you anticipated it. The weak was absorbing the strong, completely unaware that the strong could eat it up from within. But this time, only a selective seed of the strong.

Stetson raised no objections at all. The idea he found particularly intriguing was this: *We must find a way of preventing war without making war impossible*. For myself, I find this no paradox. In a universe without limits, life must grow through self-imposed limits. Every teaching turns on its *discipline*. And what is a discipline but a limit self-imposed for the benefits derived? My new *matrix* needs no distortion to encompass this concept.

Out of all this, one thought keeps coming back to me. I will mention it this once. It occurs to me that the most effective government is that one where the governed do not know they are being governed, but believe they govern themselves.

Your obed't farmer,
Lewis Orne.